Spell and Protect

Sheriff Witch Chronicles 1

By Belinda White

Belinda White

Chapter 1

How on earth had I let myself get talked into this?

It was bad enough having to work with a badge on again. I'd grown very used to being my own boss.

Well, technically, as sheriff—probationary sheriff, mind you—I was the boss. But I had a whole passel of people to answer to in this job.

I'd felt pretty good going into it. I mean, I was good at enforcing the law. Really, really good. And I had a built-in advantage that most law enforcement officials didn't have.

Most cops worked with virtual blinders on. They spent their days confident that the paranormal was just a deluded person's fantasy. They were wrong, of course, but they were bloody confident in their wrongness.

That wasn't the case with me. I knew the paranormal was real. The deluded people were those who failed to be open enough to see it when it looked them right in the eyes.

How did I know this? Why was I so certain of that fact?

Because I am the paranormal. Twice over, in fact. That happens when your Benandanti werewolf mother falls in love with a Water Elemental witch.

It makes me rather singularly able to see the truth of things. Of course, right now, that wasn't such a blessing. Right now, I kind of wished I had a set of those blinders myself.

Because I really didn't like what I was staring down at. Not one tiny little bit. I closed my eyes and said a quick prayer to my Goddess before glancing back up at the officer behind me.

The one who had called me to report the dead body in the woods. My first official night on the job and I'd already caught a dead body.

Lucky me, huh?

"Who found him?"

Deputy Tad Wallace, who was pointedly not looking at the body, nodded to a woman dressed in running gear off to the side. That nod was a silent one. I could tell the man was having trouble holding it together right now.

I stood and put a hand on his shoulder, leaning down to whisper in his ear. "If you have to get sick, try to make it at least twenty feet away from the body, okay? And don't worry about it. It happens."

It did, too. Especially with one this bad.

The deputy in question was fairly new to the team. Not quite as new as me, but close. I could tell he was struggling. Kind of figured he thought it would look bad on him if he got sick over his first body. I'd be sure to tell him later the story of my first. That should put the man at ease a bit. It hadn't been my most stellar of moments.

As I crossed over the running path to the woman he'd nodded to, I could hear him running off into the trees. Good man. He'd be able to think clearer once he got his stomach emptied out. Thinking was important in this job.

I held my hand out to the woman. "I'm Patricia Bluespring, the new probationary sheriff."

She stared at my hand for a few seconds before taking it. I didn't think it was a sign of disrespect. More likely, the woman was still in shock.

Who wouldn't be? It wasn't every night you ran across a dead body on your moonlight run. Thank the Goddess.

"Fran Michaels," she said. Then she took her hand back from the weak clasp and started hugging herself again.

"Do you run here every night?"

She shook her head. "Only once a week. I try to alternate paths for safety. I'm really wishing I hadn't pulled this one out of the hat tonight."

I raised an eyebrow. Smart woman. If one was

going to go running alone every night, it was a good thing not to follow a nightly routine. That could put a target on your head fairly easily. So at least I knew the woman had a brain. That was a good thing.

"Did you know him?"

Fran shook her head, then looked away. "I'm sorry, but I just couldn't…"

I knew what that meant, even if she couldn't bring herself to say it. She hadn't looked closely enough to tell whether she knew the man or not. It wasn't like someone would have to check to see if he was still alive.

Yeah. It was that bad. And no, I'm not going to give a detailed explanation as to why. You'll just have to trust my opinion on this one.

I took her through her movement of the night. No, she hadn't seen anyone else on the path. No, she hadn't heard or seen anything suspicious. That wasn't too unusual at this time of night. Most people did their running while the sun was still up. Especially if they were female and running alone.

Maybe the woman wasn't quite as smart as I'd at first thought.

After that, I got her address and phone number and let her go home. By then, the rest of my team and the coroner were starting to arrive.

Time to get to work. And maybe think about rethinking my current career choice.

Because Fran Michaels might not have taken a

close look at that man, but I had.

And I knew him, too.

This was so not good.

***

The victim in question was Vinnie George, and for once my grandfather's advice of not trusting anyone with two first names was right on the money.

Vinnie was not a good person. Unfortunately, he was a good hunter. Too good. Especially when one of his favorite creatures of all to hunt, legal or not, was the wolf.

For a good long while, we wolves—and yes, I was counting myself among them as I too wore that gray fur coat at times—had enjoyed the protection of being on the endangered species list. Being on that list had meant that killing a wolf was an illegal activity. Unless, of course, it was a life or death matter. Which, unless you were dealing with a rabid wolf, wasn't very likely to be the case.

Wolves get a bad rap sometimes. A totally unfounded bad rap, too. We were so much more gentle and rational than our human counterparts. For instance, wolves hunted only for survival. Not for the sport of it. Killing was a necessity of life, not a pleasure.

Unfortunately, our place on that list was now in question, and killing wolves was back in the somewhat legal range. Legal enough for Vinnie, anyway. Maybe not for most of the population, thank the Goddess.

"You thinking he got too close to a pack of wolves, and they attacked him?" Deputy Tad asked.

I had to tamper down my outrage a bit. Being rational and calm right now was important, even if the world seemed to be spinning a bit faster around me at the moment. "No," I answered. "Wolves don't carry guns the last time I checked."

The deputy glanced at the body, or at least what he could see of it, what with the coroner partially blocking our view. "You think he was shot?"

"I'm thinking that's what took the man down, yes." I hated myself for it, but it needed to be said. As hard as it was, I had to be unbiased on this one. Being unbiased was important when one was wearing a sheriff's badge. "We'll have to wait on the coroner's report as to what actually killed him, though. Could go either way on that one."

He swallowed hard a couple of times. I found myself hoping that he'd sufficiently emptied his stomach already. I really liked my new work boots, dang it. And some smells lasted longer than others. Especially to those of us born with super sniffers.

I glanced back at the crowd that was forming behind us. "I think maybe you need to give Phil a hand keeping that crowd back." He nodded, gratefully I thought, and headed further back away from the crime scene.

That was the thing about small-town life. You wouldn't think that a body in the woods would draw a crowd in the middle of the night. In most places, it wouldn't. Here in Wind's Crossing, it did. We had residents that thought listening to the police scanner was high entertainment. And once something like this went on the air, it didn't take long for the news to spread and the crowd to form.

It was sad, really. Some days I wished I wore the fur coat all the time. Dealing with humans was ever so much harder than dealing with wolves.

More dangerous, too.

I'd given the coroner a good half hour already with the body. Professional courtesy, that. I knew how much I hated trying to do my job with someone hovering over my shoulder. Kind of stood to reason others felt the same way.

Crossing the few feet between us, I knelt beside the man. "What do you have so far?"

He glanced over at me with a grim smile. "Not as much as I'll have once I get him back to the lab, but from what I can tell, the man's been dead for about four hours." He glanced at his watch. "I'd put the time of death roughly around eight o'clock. Give or take an hour."

I nodded. "So it was still daylight, then." Early May in Michigan meant it didn't start getting dark until around nine.

The coroner glanced up at the tree canopy overhead and the full moon above that. "It was probably pretty dark here in the woods, in between the sun and the moon. No street lights here." He shook his head. "What on bloody earth was that woman doing out running the path at this time of night?"

All I could do was shrug. I understood more than most the sheer pleasure of running in the woods by the light of the full moon. Of course, I was usually wearing fur when I did that.

Not exactly something I felt like sharing at the moment.

Chapter 2

It was hard to concentrate, with things being what they were. I owed it to my pack to alert them to this unfortunate occurrence.

There was a very good reason for that. Any time there was a death with even the possibility of a wolf involvement, the Luparri would show up sooner rather than later.

That meant a greatly elevated danger to my fellow Benandanti pack members.

Most people don't know about the Luparri. We did. Trust me, when you have an entire organization whose sole purpose in existence was to eradicate your entire species, you knew about them.

You did if you lived long enough, anyway.

Lucky for our kind, we have our own organization to keep tabs on them. Ours is much more benevolent and forgiving.

We don't hunt down their members and execute them with extreme prejudice. They don't, however, extend that same courtesy to us.

If you wear an occasional fur coat, to the Luparri, you are somehow equated to Satan's Spawn. That wasn't true, in any shape or form, but it was the false truth that they all held very firmly in their hearts and minds. Trying to change someone like that wasn't easy. At all.

The Benandanti came down on the side of good versus evil. We were the Goodwalkers, dang it all. Even if we couldn't get the hard-headed Luparri to acknowledge that fact.

But bottom line, I was looking at a possible wolf kill here. It sure as heck didn't help that the man was a known wolf-hunter. Put a sentient spin on the whole killing right there.

This wouldn't be one that the Luparri would pass on.

My worker bees were busy processing the scene and gathering any evidence they could. And the coroner was getting ready to release the body for transport back to his lab. A few more minutes, and I should be able to break away and make the call.

At least, that's what could have happened before I looked up and saw Steve Brighton jogging down the path toward my crime scene. Normally, that would be a sight I wouldn't mind seeing.

The man was a rather fine specimen of manliness, all in all. And he looked mighty good in that uniform of his, too.

No, it wasn't a Wind's Crossing Sheriff uniform. The man was a deputy all right, but not in my county or jurisdiction. He was from Oak Hill.

Steve and I went back a way. In fact, the two of us had been dating on and off again for about a year now.

The only problem with that?

I was fairly certain that Steve Brighton was an official card-carrying member of the Luparri.

So why was I dating a man who would most likely kill me the instant he learned I was a Benandanti werewolf? Well, part of it was the fact that it was smart to keep your friends close and your enemies closer. That saying was true in a lot of ways. Especially in this circumstance.

But it went beyond that, too. Goddess help me, but I liked the man. Really, really liked him. He didn't fit the mold of an evil and sadistic werewolf hunter to me.

And for me, that meant there had to be a way to help him see the light. I was really hoping that would be possible.

I just wished it didn't take me risking my life and the lives of my pack mates to do that.

Deputy Wallace earned a bit more of my respect when he stepped out in front of the man, hindering his progress toward me. As I said, Steve might be in uniform, but it wasn't one of ours.

As I watched, they exchanged words, then

both of them looked at me. My call. I gave a curt nod. It's not like I could keep this out of his reach for long.

He finished the short distance at a slower pace. His eyes never stopped moving, either. The man was good at his job. I didn't think much would get by him.

If there had been anything much to see, that was. There wasn't.

Not much to smell, either. Other than what you'd expect at a scene like this one. Even a wolf like me with a super sniffer would have a hard time sorting through all the scents along this path.

It was mushroom season in Michigan, and the woods had been crawling with their hunters for a few weeks now. Every one of them hoping to take home a sack to enjoy or sell. Morels didn't come cheap at the market.

And yes, I was trying to calm and distract myself by thinking of something other than the crisis at hand.

I stepped out a few feet from the actual crime scene to meet him halfway.

"Hope you don't mind me barging in like this," he said. "I was actually on my way to your place to congratulate you on your first official day as sheriff when I heard the call on the radio."

That made sense. I'd wondered how he had gotten there so blasted fast. It was kind of nice, too.

"Probationary sheriff."

"Huh?" He'd been looking behind me at the coroner and the body. When I spoke, he dragged his eyes back to me.

"I'm just the probationary sheriff. A six-month trial before they make it official."

He blinked at me, then smiled. "I'm pretty sure those six months won't make any difference to your new title. Well, other than dropping that probationary part of it."

Funny, but with the case currently in front of me, I wasn't nearly so sure that would be the end result. Either way, it was fine by me. I was beginning to think maybe I'd made a mistake taking this darn job to begin with. But the Taylors can be very persuading when they wanted to be.

And neither of the Taylor men wanted to keep the position. I was starting to see why, too.

"You mind if I take a look?"

I swallowed. Did I mind? Heck yes. The last thing I wanted to do was give an agent of the Luparii a reason to go on a wolf hunt. I had every reason in the book to stop him from crossing that line onto the scene, too.

He was way out of his jurisdiction here.

Unfortunately, there was such a thing as professional courtesy. He obviously thought that applied here. Also unfortunately, I thought he was probably right.

Taking a deep breath, I stepped to the side and

allowed him past.

Once again, his eyes were everywhere. But after only a cursory glance at the body and a nod to the coroner, he knelt down to survey the ground.

I knew that move. I'd done it enough times in my day. He was in full-on tracking mode.

"Anything worth sharing?" I asked.

He shook his head. "Not that I can see." He scrubbed at his cheek for a minute, then reached down to spread the grass beneath his fingers. Nothing there.

Good thing, too. How embarrassing would that have been? Being shown up by another department on my first official night on the job?

The one thing I had going for me, with the whole Luparii thing, was that it had been dry the past few days. Dry, packed dirt really wasn't the greatest when it came time to track someone. Or something. Like a wolf.

Of course, that was also a bad thing when it came to tracking the killer as a sheriff.

Not that I was saying this had been a wolf. It could well have been a large dog. There were several of them in the area. People out here believed in protecting their property. Big dogs helped with that.

Come to think of it, a lot of people ran with their dogs, didn't they? Maybe that wasn't such a stretch after all.

Finally, he stood back up, brushing his hands against his thighs. Muscular thighs, too. There was more than one reason I was interested in this man.

"You and your men find anything yet?"

I shook my head. "Nothing to give any indication of who did this." I nodded to the body as the coroner stepped back to allow the workers to start the transporting process. "He was shot. That much is clear. Pretty sure that's what took him down."

I hesitated, but what could it hurt to throw it out there? "People run this path. Some do it with their dogs. Could have been an altercation, then their dog took action too."

His eyes narrowed, but he nodded slowly. "Could be."

Yeah, I wasn't sure that was the case, either. Would have been a lot more believable if the man on the ground hadn't been a known wolf-hunter. That kind of changed things when you weren't wearing those magical blinders.

And I was pretty sure that the Luparii collected those things at the door.

Chapter 3

The coroner's team took the body back to the lab, and my men and I set about canvassing the area for any clues that the killer might have left behind. Of course, the popularity of this trail hindered that process a great deal.

Anything we found could well have been dropped by the killer, or any one of a few hundred mushroom hunters. Kind of hard to narrow that down, too.

By the time the sun finally started making its presence known with actual daylight filtering through the trees overhead, we'd done all we could. Unfortunately, we were no better off than we were when we'd started.

In other words, we had absolute zilch. Nada. Nothing. Not a brilliant start to an illustrious career as a sheriff.

As my men started packing all our lights and equipment up, Steve turned to me. "Well, that's that then." He hesitated. "It's too late for the midnight dinner I had planned for us, but we could always make that a breakfast, if you're interested."

I thought about it. But the man had two things going against him. One, I was absolutely exhausted. And two, I had a lot of calls to make before I was going to be able to get any actual rest.

"I'm thinking I'll have to take a rain check on that for tonight. Or, well, today." After all, it was day now… wasn't it?

He nodded. "I can understand that." He looked away. "You going to be pulling the evening shift for a while?"

Yeah, that's why it hadn't struck me as odd, the man heading to my place in the middle of the night. I'd let him know about my new hours upfront. One does that for the man in their life.

"That's the plan. As much as hours are scheduled for a probationary sheriff, that is. I'm pretty much on call all the time now." Yet another reason I was wondering why I'd agreed to the position. The Taylor men must be even more persuasive than I'd thought.

Steve rubbed the back of his neck, still not meeting my eyes. "Can I ask you something?"

Dagnabbit, but I hated it when people asked that. I mean, what could you say? No?

"Guess it's hard for me to give you an answer without knowing what the question is, isn't it?"

"Yeah." He took a deep breath. "Is this sheriff thing going to change things? I mean, between us?"

I just looked at him. I could see the wolf thing changing things between us—big time—but the sheriff thing? "No. Why would it?"

He shrugged. "You know, you being a sheriff and me being just a deputy."

All I could do was blink at him. "First of all, in my honest opinion, there is no such thing as 'just a deputy'. Deputies put their lives on the line just as often as sheriffs do. Maybe even more so. And second, you don't work for me."

His gaze finally met mine, searchingly. After a minute, he nodded. "Good. I just wanted to be sure it wouldn't make it awkward for us."

"Not for me." Then I paused. "Does it for you?" Men could be so weird about the balance of power thing sometimes. Current case in point. I mean, this whole thing had never even crossed my mind once.

He shook his head. "I don't think so. But it will take some getting used to."

I didn't much care for the sound of that. If the situation had been reversed, I truly doubted he'd be having any issue with a sheriff dating a deputy from a different precinct. I just might be dealing with a bit of a chauvinist here.

I didn't much care for chauvinists, either.

Steve left shortly after that, and yes, I realized

I might have misspoken. The sheriff thing could indeed make things awkward between us, if that was how he felt about things. Only time would tell.

Wanting to make a statement without actually saying anything, I stayed until the last of my men had left the scene to head back to the station to clock out and go home. I believed in showing them I was going to put my all into the job, and that generally meant putting in more hours than anyone else.

Not that there would be much choice in the matter with the title of sheriff.

By the time I made it back to my car, my body was telling me I'd better make those calls pretty snappy because it would not be able to keep me on my feet—or my backside for that matter—much longer.

Good thing I had Bluetooth set up in my car, huh? I could drive and talk at the same time.

Legally, too.

***

Okay, so it's confession time. I know I talk a lot about 'my' pack and pack mates. But the truth is, I'm not truly a member of any pack. Not officially, anyway.

The problem isn't that I'm only half Benandanti, either. As that gene was only passed down by the mother, that was the case with a lot of werewolves. Most of them had regular, everyday human fathers. That wasn't an issue.

The problem was that I was half elemental witch.

Witches and wolves went back a long, long way. They weren't always as friendly toward each other as they are now. In fact, in the early days, the Benandanti had pretty much seen witches as the evil enemy. A few bad seeds had started it, but it was hard to prove ourselves afterward and gain their trust.

It was also hard to forget the hunts and attacks the wolves went on before coming to the realization that, just maybe, all witches weren't all bad. A lot of innocent witches died in those attacks.

That's kind of hard to forget.

Even today, some wolves didn't much care for witches and vice versa. Just lucky me that I had to deal with both sides on a regular basis. That happens when you have the blood of both running through your veins. Makes you a bit of an outsider with each side too.

There was also the whole Alpha and Beta thing, too. I was an Alpha wolf, and I didn't really relish the idea of blindly following a leader just because the pack said they were in charge. Yeah, I guess that makes me a bit of a lone wolf.

But back to the matter at hand. I stared at my phone for a long minute, trying to decide where to start. The obvious choice was to call the local Alpha couple. As far as packs go, the local one wasn't so bad. They'd come to me a time or two for help with certain delicate matters, and as a result, had taken me into the peripheral fold of their pack. I was kind of an honorary pack member.

They did the same for some of the other non-pack Alphas in the area, too. Allowed them to join in monthly meetings to stay abreast with the area news. It was something they didn't have to do, but something we were all grateful for all the same.

As I said, the local pack wasn't so bad. But even as my finger was ready to press the first digit of their number, Gray popped into my head. Alerting him wouldn't be a bad idea either.

He was the new leader of the Bear's Creek pack. And a friend to boot. Plus, alerting him would also take care of alerting the Ravenswind witches. That wouldn't be a bad idea, either. Especially since two of them were mated to the Taylor ex-sheriffs. I just might need all their help with this one.

Which brought up my third possibility, and my fingers did their thing.

"Orville Taylor here."

"Hey, Orville, it's Patty." I hesitated. It was still very early in the morning. A fact I had, until now, conveniently forgotten. "I hope I didn't wake you."

He chuckled. "Don't worry about it. Sleeping in is for sissies. What can I do for you?"

I told him the situation as briefly as I could. And no, I didn't leave anything out. Orville was one of the few everyday humans who'd had his blinders yanked off a couple of years ago. He knew about the 'other' side of things.

"I see," he said. "What can I do to help?"

I thought about it. I'd been so sure that he was the right one to call first, but now that he asked... why had I thought that? What did I want from him?

"I'm not sure, really. Maybe just keep your ear to the ground for me? Let me know if you learn anything of interest?" I paused. "And I would appreciate it if you'd let Gray know, too. He can pass the news on to his pack as well. That'll save me some time."

"I can do that." He went silent for a minute. "And Patty?"

"Yeah, Orville?"

"Watch yourself out there, okay?"

I swallowed. For a long, long time I'd been pretty much on my own in the world. Now I had friends. Good people, too. People who said things like that and really, truly meant them. It felt good.

"I will, and thanks."

"For what?"

"Just being you." And then, before I could let my exhausted and overburdened self get any mushier, I hung up.

One call down, and one to go.

Chapter 4

In the end, it wasn't a call I made. At least, not over the phone.

Even as tired as I was, this situation required more of me. So, I headed to the nearest convenience store and filled up on coffee. One cup for now, and yet another as standby for my drive home. I'd need them both before I made it to bed.

And by then, I'd be so bloody tired that the extra caffeine would not mean diddly squat.

The Alpha couple didn't live all that far from my little A-frame. At least that part of things worked in my favor. When I pulled up in front of their house, I could see lights on inside. Yet another thing in my favor.

Hopefully, that string of luck would continue.

Damon Nichols was, by day, an accountant. A busy one this time of year, wrapping up everyone's taxes and getting back to the normal everyday work routine, and all those jobs that had been put on hold during tax time. I'd counted on him being up and moving already, but I breathed a lot easier when I saw those lights on, all the same.

One does not want to go waking an Alpha wolf from his restful slumber unless one has absolutely no choice in the matter. They aren't Alpha's for nothing.

I got out of my car and walked to the door. Slowly. I needed the added time to gather my thoughts. How did I handle this in a way that came across as non-aggressive while still letting the man know that anyone in the pack would now be considered a major suspect?

Talk about walking a thin line. This was it.

Taking a deep breath, I ignored the doorbell and knocked. If his wife, Celia, was still sleeping, maybe it would be best if she continued to do so. The two of us, both being Alpha females, had clashed a time or two in the past. Nothing that we hadn't been able to work through. For the most part, anyway. But grudges ran deep with some.

I had a feeling Celia was a woman with a lot of very deep grudges running through her veins. And truthfully? I just wasn't sure I was up to dealing with her attitude after the night I'd just been through.

Damon's look of annoyance changed immediately to dread when he opened the door and saw me standing there. Yeah, having a sheriff show up on your doorstep this early in the morning couldn't exactly be good news, could it?

"Damon." I nodded to him. "I wondered if you had a minute to talk."

He never hesitated, but his gaze went up the stairs as he stepped to the side to let me in. "Do I need to wake Celia?"

I shook my head. "Not at this point. I'll let you fill her in on this later." I knew that was just me taking the easy way out, but again, even I had my limits as to what I could bear within a twenty-four-hour period.

We ended up in their living room. A comfortable enough space, if a tad rustic for me. They took the whole living in a log cabin thing to the extreme, if you asked me. No matter where you were in their home, you always knew you were in a log cabin.

A huge log cabin, mind you, but a log cabin all the same. It was a point of pride to them. Though, for the life of me, I couldn't understand why.

I waited for him to sit before taking a chair myself. Official member of the pack or not, I owed him that sign of respect. Then I looked into his eyes. "Vinnie George's body was found this morning on the jogging path that goes through the park in Wind's Crossing. There are signs of wolf involvement in the death."

His eyes widened, and he stood to pace back and forth, a string of curses coming from him. Muffled curses, yes, in deference to his sleeping wife upstairs, but curses. Imaginative ones, too.

If I'd been a full pack member, I'd have stood back up when he did. The mind was willing, but my body was just about at its end of productive use. I continued to sit. If he noticed the breach of protocol, he didn't mention it.

Part of that could have been the uniform I was wearing. After all, a sheriff was due some signs of respect, too.

I didn't say a word. Just let him pace back and forth for a couple of minutes. Finally, he stopped and stared at me. "What kind of signs of wolf involvement?"

"Definite bite marks on the body. Whether or not they contributed to the actual cause of death, I don't know yet. It will be the coroner's job to determine that. The man had been shot, too. With any luck, the bullet will be what killed him."

Damon nodded. He knew exactly what I was saying. If a bite was the cause of death, then we were definitely looking at a wolf. If it was the bullet... well, that opened things up to a more hopeful note, anyway.

"Kind of need to know information, that," he said dryly.

I had to agree. Glancing at my watch, I realized that the coroner just might be able to tell me that by now. I made the call.

When I left the Nichols' home a few minutes later, pretty much dead on my feet, at least my heart was a little lighter.

Vinnie George had been killed by a bullet directly piercing his heart. According to the coroner, death would have been pretty much instant.

That, coupled with the fact that I was fairly certain my telling Damon was the first he'd heard of it, gave me just enough strength to make it home.

Well, that and the second cup of coffee.

***

As I'd agreed to take the evening shift at the station, I wasn't due in at the office until six o'clock that night. But that timeframe flew right out the window whenever there was an active murder investigation.

One of the bad things about being sheriff? It was a salary position. No overtime. That part of it wasn't exactly fair, especially with the pittance of a salary the position drew for the job and the hours it entailed.

Good thing I was in it more for the justice of things than for the money, huh? Yeah, if money had been my prime motivator for a job, law enforcement would not have been my first career choice.

It was a calling, more than anything. Some were called to serve the Lord. Others were called to serve their country. I was called to serve the law.

That motto of Serve and Protect meant

something to me. Although, with me, it was more of a Spell and Protect kind of thing. Same difference in the end, I thought.

I'd set my alarm to give me a blessed four hours of sleep. I made it to three and a half before my phone was ringing.

"Sheriff Bluespring."

"Sorry to bother you so early, Sheriff, but we've been fending off reporters all morning."

It was Trevor Taylor. My number one deputy, as it were. Not that any of my people were shabby, mind you. Orville and Trevor had already weeded the bad ones out long before I took the reins.

"They are getting more insistent. I kind of promised them a press conference at noon. Do you think you can make that? If not, I can pinch hit for you, but I'd kind of like to know how you want to handle it first."

I groaned. Yet another perk that came with the title of sheriff. Dealing with reporters. It was very tempting to ask Trevor to handle the press conference, but I didn't think that would show too good of a face to the general public. Not with how new I was to the job and all.

"I can make it." I glanced at the clock. That gave me a whopping half an hour. And it was a twenty-minute drive into Wind's Crossing, even if I didn't much pay attention to the speed limit along the way. After a second's hesitation, I added, "If I'm running a few minutes late, stall them for me, okay?"

"You got it."

I was already up and on my way to the restroom, but I had to ask. "I don't suppose any miracles happened in the last few hours that broke the case wide open?"

He chuckled. "Sorry, Sheriff. Afraid we're going to have to work for this one."

"Yeah, well, it was worth the thought. See you soon."

I hung up, took care of the immediate necessities of nature, then ran a washcloth over my face and a brush through my hair. I blinked at the reflection staring back at me in the mirror.

It wasn't the most stellar of looks, but luckily, I wasn't the kind of woman that wore a ton of makeup. More like none. The closest I came to it was when I applied a bit of Chapstick when my lips got dry. With the odd hours, that was a good thing.

Within ten minutes of getting the call, I was on the road.

That should have given me time to get to the station before the press circus started. Technically, it did, as I got there right at noon, straight up. Trevor was just stepping up to the podium in front of the reporters when I walked in.

I could see the look of relief in his eyes when he saw me walk through the door. Yeah, I don't think there was ever a lawman born that enjoyed dealing with reporters. Not the ones that were worth their salt, anyway.

We got lucky that it wasn't a packed house. There were only six reporters in total. The only thing that made me blink twice was the sight of that blasted video camera. I could handle photos. That came with the job. However, the thought of being on television, even in a brief news clip, wasn't a happy one.

I was regretting not letting Trevor handle this.

That was one thing my previous job as enforcer for the Witch's Council had going for it. We pretty much stayed out of the limelight. No press meetings for us.

This would take some getting used to.

And just maybe I wasn't as cut out for this job as I'd thought I was.

Chapter 5

The press conference went as well as it could go, for the most part.

Things got a little dicey there for a few seconds when one of the reporters asked point-blank if it had been a rogue wolf attack. I answered with the truth.

History doesn't show a single case of an unprovoked wolf attack against a human. It just isn't in their nature. Then I followed that up by asking them about the last time they had seen a wolf in that park. And then followed that up by asking how often they saw people running with large dogs.

They got the message pretty quick, and I was off the hook. With the press, at least.

It was a really good thing we werewolves were still firmly in our little closet, or things would have gone a lot differently.

Witches weren't the only ones that had problems with the general public in earlier times. In

Europe, there had been werewolf trials too. Trials every bit as bad as the witch trials of Salem here in America. To include the whole burning at the stake thing.

I really didn't like the thought of those starting back up again. Hopefully, I'd be able to prove a normal, one hundred percent human being had killed Vinnie George. In fact, that was what I was counting on. Pretty dang heavily, too.

The other path just wasn't one I was ready to think about yet. If a werewolf had killed Vinnie, then we probably were looking at a Melandanti. We Benandantis were the Goddess's Good Walkers. The Melandanti? Not so much. Kind of our exact opposite, really.

If that were the case, then this could very well just be the beginning. Things were likely to go downhill pretty dang fast, too. The Luparri already had a presence here. If a Melandanti really was on the loose? That presence would only grow.

Not good for the Benandantis in the area. At all. We know the difference. The Luparri do not. To them, every being capable of shifting to another form is evil. Therefore, they need to be eradicated or, in simpler terms, assassinated. Shoot first and ask questions never.

I will not lie and say I've never killed in the past. I have. But only when there was absolutely no other choice in the matter. Evil witches and

Melandanti werewolves rarely gave you the choice to allow them to live.

Of course, that might not be the worst of things. The world was definitely a better place without them in it. And they had far too many secrets to allow them to be held in human jails. It's just the way it was.

I heard voices in the hallway. I might have an office, tiny as it was, but that didn't mean I normally shut the door. A sheriff should be accessible to her deputies, I thought.

Glancing up, I smiled when I recognized the visitor that Trevor was bringing in to see me. Gray.

Gray was the newest Alpha pack leader of the Bear's Creek pack. Doing a bang-up job of it, too. Especially as he had bucked the norms and chosen to not take a werewolf for a mate. That was a hard sell, and it just went to show how very much that pack needed a good leader. They had been willing to change a long-standing tradition to have him in charge.

He was a very reluctant leader, yes, but since he'd accepted the role, the man was determined to do right by his pack. The pack had chosen wisely. Gray was a vast improvement on their last Alpha male.

I stood and walked around my desk, holding out my hand. He brushed it to one side and gathered me in a fierce hug. Trust the man to know I needed that right now. I could feel a portion of his strength pouring into me.

This having close friends thing—almost to the point of them being family—was still fairly new to me. It was also really, really nice. Having someone take your back was a very good feeling.

It made you a heck of a lot safer, too.

As he leaned in for the hug, he whispered, "I thought maybe we should have a joint pack conference?"

He wasn't whispering because of Trevor. Trevor knew our dirty little secret.

He should. He'd been there when I'd let the secret out by turning to his mate and him for help when I'd been shot. If it hadn't been for them, I'd have bled to death in the woods. At the time, a hospital was kind of out of the question.

But the rest of the station? Yeah. This would be a closed-door meeting for sure.

***

As it turned out, it was an outdoor meeting.

In my rush to get to the press conference in time, I hadn't had a chance to eat anything. My body was telling me I needed to rectify that situation. Fast.

It wasn't good to be hungry as a human. I got that. But it was doubly worse to be hungry as a wolf. And even though I may wear skin rather than fur most of the time, that didn't mean I wasn't still a wolf on the inside.

A very hungry wolf at the moment.

We headed to the market and picked up deli sandwiches and chips and then went to the little gazebo at the center of Wind's Crossing to eat. It was the best place to have a private conversation.

That fact might surprise you, but it was true. Indoors, at least in any public place, there was always the chance of being overheard. Someone standing around the corner. The walls not being as thick as you'd like to think they were. Or someone just out and out eavesdropping on the sheriff because they wanted the latest news for the rumor mill.

Needless to say, the conversation we were about to have wasn't one we could risk being overheard.

The three of us, Gray, Trevor, and I, settled onto the picnic table in the middle of the large, open gazebo. Luckily, the place was empty except for us. And with me sitting on one side of the table and the men on the other, we'd know pretty dang quickly if that changed, too.

"I don't like this one bit," Gray said before taking a bite of his sub.

I nodded. "Neither do I."

Trevor looked from one of us to the other, an odd look on his face. "This is about the fact that Vinnie George was a wolf hunter, isn't it?" His face lost a little color. "Please tell me you don't think a werewolf did this? I thought you all were the good guys."

Gray met my eyes over the table. "Yeah, well, ninety-nine percent of us are. But there are exceptions to every rule," he said.

Trevor swallowed. "Crap."

Yup. That pretty much summed it up. All in one word. Crap.

Trevor paused and then looked me in the eye. "That still didn't really answer my question, you know."

I swallowed the huge bite I'd just taken and then chased it down with a drink to give myself time to think of how to respond. This was Trevor we were talking about. He deserved nothing but the truth.

No matter how damaging that truth might be.

"If the victim had been anyone other than Vinnie George, I'd say in no uncertain terms that I didn't think a werewolf was involved." Then I paused. "Of course, I could have been wrong, even then. Just as not all humans are good, not all weres are either."

Gray nodded. "Unfortunately, that's the way of it. That other one percent has caused us Benandantis a heck of a lot of grief in the past." He glanced at me again. "Do you think that's what we're dealing with? The Melandanti?"

"The Melandanti?" Trevor asked.

I glanced at Trevor. "The Melandanti is that one percent Gray was talking about. Although, it's more like a tenth of one percent... if even that." Then my eyes went back to Gray, and I lifted a shoulder. "I hope not, but it's always a possibility. But there's another possibility too."

Both men were looking at me now. I had their full and undivided attention.

"Let's face it, guys. Vinnie hunted wolves. Legally, illegally, it just didn't matter to him much. If it wore a wolf's coat, it was fair game to him. And all of us know that not all wolves stay in fur form."

Gray frowned. "You think he killed one of us?"

I shook my head. "Not killed, no. I would like to think I would have heard of that happening. But what's to say he hadn't tracked one of us to our homes and started the stalking process?"

Trevor blanched even more. "Double crap."

"Yeah, well, get ready to triple it, because it gets even worse," I told him. "You remember me telling you about the Luparri?"

He rubbed his forehead as if in sudden pain. "They'll get involved in this, won't they?"

I glanced at Gray before answering. "Unless I'm mistaken, they already are."

Gray's eyes sharpened on me as I'd known they would. "What do you know that I don't?"

"First, I need your word that you won't act on what I'm about to tell you. Or tell another single soul."

I could tell he didn't much care for my terms,

but I wasn't about to budge on this one. I thought there was still hope for Steve, and I wanted the chance to prove that hunch of mine right.

Finally, he nodded. "So be it." Then he paused only a microsecond before continuing. "But if my pack is in danger, I have an obligation to protect them."

Which, unfortunately, put the ball directly back into my court. In the end, it all boiled down to whether or not I trusted Gray with the truth.

Come to find out, I did.

Chapter 6

There was a great thing about having a competent ex-sheriff on your payroll. With Trevor there, I basically had the ability to split the investigation right down the middle.

And know that neither part would go wanting. That was the important thing. I'd seen what Trevor was capable of. He was good. Really good. The town had done well, making him their interim sheriff. It hadn't just been the father and son thing some had thought it was.

I put him in charge of doing interviews with all the friends, family, and associates of Vinnie George. The normal side of things. After all, it was entirely possible that the large dog story I'd sold to the press just might be true.

Mind you, I wasn't betting that was the case. But it could be true, all the same.

What all that meant was that I was more freed up to do my thing. I called in a favor of my friend

Opal Ravenswind, High Priestess of the local Gemstone Coven, and got permission to borrow her hilltop for the evening. She assured me that I would have full privacy up there.

That privacy thing was paramount. With all the Benandantis in the hot seat right now, it simply wouldn't be safe to have a meeting in a public place, like the parks we usually gathered in for our monthly runs. Especially when this would be a joint pack meeting. Double the wolves.

Emotions, and possibly tempers, were likely to be high during this one. And no, I hadn't told either pack about the other one attending. Neither had Gray.

There was a reason wolves generally stuck to their own packs.

But with a murder right smack in the middle of the two packs' territories? Yeah. Something had to give. Hopefully, they'd be able to put their differences aside for a short time. At least until we put the killer behind bars.

All I could do was hope that the killer wouldn't be a were from one of the two packs I'd be meeting with. But either way, murder is murder—and had to be dealt with as such. Messy as that might be in this case.

I'd made sure that the invitation said two things plainly. One, attendance was mandatory. And two, eat before you come.

That second one might not seem like all that

big of a deal, but when you're dealing with wolves, it is. A hungry wolf simply isn't a very rational—or stable—wolf. I was really hoping they'd take that seriously and have a whole lot of meat in their systems before showing up to find the meeting wasn't just for their pack.

If there's one thing that can mellow out a wolf, it's a belly full of meat. Trust me on that.

My pack arrived, as planned, at seven o'clock sharp. I knew that Damon and Celia ran a tight ship, and they didn't disappoint me. Everyone was present and accounted for. That was good.

They weren't thrilled, however, when I didn't immediately start the meeting. It didn't take long for them to realize I'd set them up.

Things got worse when Gray and the Bear's Creek pack showed up ten minutes later.

"What the devil are they doing here?" Celia growled. And yes, I do mean growled. The growl was so prominent, in fact, that the words kind of slurred. The meaning and her expression, however, were clear.

"They are here because I called them here. As sheriff of Wind's Crossing. This is a legal matter, and for just this once, our packs are going to have to work together. Believe me when I say that will be of benefit to both packs."

Celia turned a beet-red face to me. I noticed that, thus far, Damon had remained silent. At least I had that much going for me.

"Nothing that pack of inbreed pups has to offer will benefit our pack." Then she motioned behind her. All her wolves stood. "We're leaving."

She left me with no choice. An alpha was an alpha, yes. But a sheriff was a bloody sheriff, too.

I stepped right up to her. "No, you are not. I am the law here, and you will sit your fanny down and listen to me. This is too important of an issue we have to deal with tonight to draw pack lines."

She lifted a hand but before I could stop her strike, Damon did. Probably a good thing. I couldn't have let a thing like that go. Most likely, he respected that fact. Whereas to Celia, it didn't mean a dang thing.

"Stop," he said. "We stay."

Damon pulled a furious Celia to the right of the hilltop clearing. It might be a joint meeting, but the packs were definitely keeping their distance from each other.

That was more than fine by me.

I glanced over at Gray. "Is this all of your pack?"

He swallowed, then shook his head. "All but two. Donnie and Nell Adams are out of touch. His office said he took a... vacation."

That pause told me that there was more to the story. It also told me that it wasn't something he wanted to share with the entire group. For what it's worth, I thought he was most likely right on that.

"Might I ask what's going on?" That was a female from Gray's pack. "Why the joint meeting? You don't really think a wolf was involved in that hunter's death, do you?"

I looked her in the eyes, then did the same with every wolf there. "As a matter of fact, I'm afraid it's looking like that might very well be the case. So I'm going to need to know where each and every one of you was last night between the hours of seven and nine. And I'll need to know if anyone can back that up, too."

Celia started to say something, but I just held up a hand to her. She glared at me but closed her trap all the same. Damon's grip on her knee might have helped that happen.

"I'm not quite finished. We also need to know if any of you are aware of wolves in the area not associated with a pack. Or any new packs, for that matter." I looked out over the packs. "And finally, I need to make you all aware that the Luparri is most likely not going to pass this one by. Be on your guard. Watch your shifts and travel in pairs at the least when you go for runs."

They didn't much like that last part, but it was important to state all the same. A lone wolf was a wolf in danger.

With Gray's help, it didn't take all that long. I worked my way through my pack, and he worked his way through his. We met, as it were, in the middle.

Most of the wolves we talked with had pretty solid alibis. Or at least they said they did. I'd have to be checking them out, of course. But the more worrisome ones were the two that didn't.

It didn't help that one of those two was Celia Nichols.

***

Gray and I stayed behind up on that hilltop long after the rest of our packs had left. We still had things to talk about, and you really couldn't beat the privacy of Opal's blessed hilltop. The place fairly buzzed with magic.

"So, what's up with this Donnie and Nell Adams? Are they a married couple?"

Gray shook his head. "No. Might be easier if they were. Donnie is Nell's father. It's just the two of them. The mom ran out shortly after Nell was born. Some people just aren't cut out to be parents. Nell's mom was one of them."

"Must have been tough on Donnie."

Gray was quiet for a minute, then shook his head. "Truthfully? I think that woman running off was the best thing that could have happened. For all of them. Donnie really stepped up. He's been a good dad. Responsible too. Having Nell really turned his life around. In a good way."

"You think they're really on vacation? And if

the answer to that is yes, then I'm going to be backing it up with when did they leave and where did they go?"

He gave me one of his half-smiles. "I figured that would be the case. The trouble is, I don't know. His office said he was on vacation, but when I got the girl talking, she admitted that it hadn't been pre-approved. It was a last-minute kind of thing."

"And it started....?"

"Just this morning." He took a deep breath. "I stopped by their house on my way here tonight to see if I could catch him home. No sign of either of them, and it looks like they left in a bit of a hurry, too. It's enough to have me worried."

I nodded. I got that. It had me worried too.

"I think we need to start out by finding where the two of them went. The timing is definitely suspicious."

"Agreed," he said slowly. "But finding them could prove problematic. Donnie was an old-school kind of wolf. Not really fond of technology. No cell phone, no internet. Electricity and a landline phone were big deals to him. Didn't mean he much liked either of them."

"You're saying that there won't likely be a strong trail to follow."

"Yup. Exactly that. And the scent trail isn't going to do us much good, either. They took Donnie's old beat-up pickup truck. No way to track that, either."

I grinned at him. "Yeah, it's really too bad one of us isn't a sheriff or something, isn't it?"

He blinked at me. "Well, there is that. But do you really want to put them out as suspects until we have the chance to talk with them?"

I thought about that for a few seconds. "No. But that doesn't mean my position doesn't have its perks. I'll have my most trusted deputies keep an eye out for the truck. Not to make contact, just to let me know where it is."

"I guess I'm okay with that."

I upped my grin at him. "But I think you're forgetting an even more important fact, Gray."

He squinted at me. "I am?"

"Yeah. I'm not just a sheriff. I'm a witch too."

His brow cleared. "You can do a Find spell."

I nodded. "Yup, and as much as I'd like to say it could wait until morning, I think we need to find them sooner rather than later."

"I'm with you there. Let me check in with Kim and tell her I'm going to be gone tonight. Then I'm all yours."

"Sounds good, and while you talk with Kim, I'll check with Opal and see if she has a few Find spells I can borrow. One thing about being a sheriff, it doesn't really leave a lot of time for mixing spells."

Or anything else, for that matter.

Chapter 7

Opal came through with three Find spells. Hopefully, that would be more than enough to do the job at hand. If not, well, at least it would give us a dang good head start.

Gray had misled me a bit by calling the Adams' residence a house. To my mind, that term did not apply. I stared at the structure in front of me and then over at Gray.

"This is where they live?"

He nodded.

"Is that a Hobbit hole, or what?" I asked because that's the closest way I could describe it. Before me was a tall mound of grass-covered dirt. A small hill, basically. Only this hill differed from any other hill I'd ever seen. It had a door.

Gray took a deep breath. "It's an earth-berm house. Most of it is underground. This is basically just the way inside." He shrugged. "As I told you, Donnie Adams is an old-school wolf. This was as close as he could come to actually living in a wolf den."

I have to admit, the thought of a home like this was growing on me. The earth surrounding the structure would provide excellent insulation against both extreme heat and extreme cold. And a person working the night shift, as I generally did, wouldn't have to be bothered by all the pesky bright sunlight streaming in through the windows while one tried to sleep.

It would have its advantages, for sure. But with one big possible drawback. A drawback I couldn't see a wolf like Donnie Adams letting stand.

"There's another entrance to the place, isn't there?" I asked.

He nodded. "A couple. Just don't ask me where they are. I don't have a clue. Donnie is a bit reclusive. He likes his privacy."

Yeah. The man and his daughter lived in a hole in the ground. I got that.

"All right then." I looked at Gray. "Are you doing the honors, or am I?"

He knew what I was asking. Technically, we didn't have the right to bust that front door down without a warrant. But getting a warrant in this situation wasn't something we wanted to do. Not to mention the fact that it would be practically impossible to get one without getting into the whole werewolf thing.

"I'll do it." He started gathering himself up to

rush the door.

I laid a hand on his arm. "Hold up there, Rambo. That door looks pretty dang solid."

Gray eyed the door. "That it does."

I thought for a minute, then dug out my phone. I kept a handy file of spells in its pretty substantial memory. No way could I remember all of them. It only took a minute to find what I was looking for.

A lock-free spell. I cast the spell, then nodded to Gray. "I think you'll find the door is unlocked."

He blinked at me and nodded. "I'll just bet I will." Gray strode forward and pushed the door open. Then he screamed and stumbled back, covering his face.

I rushed forward, preparing to defend us, but there was nothing. Then it hit me. I kept from screaming, but it was a very close thing.

As hard as it was, I forced myself to the door and slammed it shut again. Holding my breath the entire time. Then we jogged a good distance away so we could finally breathe again.

The two of us weren't a pretty sight right at that moment. Our glands were working overtime, trying to produce water to cleanse the situation. Drool and tears weren't really helping matters.

"The rat turd set a scent bomb booby trap," Gray gasped out.

I glanced back at the offending hill. This was the super hard part. The part where a sheriff had to step up, even when she really, really didn't want to.

That scent bomb effectively cut off any wolf's hope of getting a scent trail on the inhabitants. That bomb's scent now permeated everything. Getting a good sniff of an actual scent on either of the missing wolves simply would not be possible now.

That left the Find spell as our only hope. Only, I had to go inside to collect what I needed.

Here's the thing. Humans have a pretty good sense of smell, right? I mean, think of how bad a skunk scent smells to a human. Now take that thought and multiply it by a hundred. That's right, a hundred. Totally not exaggerating here.

There was a reason Gray had screamed when that stupid bomb activated. And now I had to find some way to work past it. This situation wasn't going away, and I hadn't been kidding about the need to find these two sooner rather than later. To me, this just made that even more certain.

I really wanted to talk with Donnie Adams right about now.

Gray was staring at me. "It'd take weeks for that place to clear out enough to go in. You know that, right?"

I nodded. Unfortunately, I didn't have weeks. One way or another, I was going in tonight. That's when I remembered the riot kit in my trunk. And the gas mask in that kit.

It most likely wouldn't completely do the job,

but it would help. Especially if I could somehow figure out how to do a fresh air spell and contain the effects of that spell within the mask itself.

I didn't get it on the first try, but within half an hour, I was walking through that front door. Even with the gas mask and spell firmly in place, it wasn't a pleasant thing to do.

And come to find out, I'd sacrificed my nose and my current clothing, which I'd for sure be burning after this, all for nothing.

Donnie Adams must have known that more than just wolves would be after him. He'd taken every strand of DNA from either of them with him.

Donnie and Nell Adams were in the wind.

***

I was going to do my level best to make it an early night, work-wise. I had leeway with my hours, as I was the top dog in the pile. Plus, it wasn't like the men hadn't seen me there at that press conference. They knew I wasn't just phoning my work in.

And truthfully? My men were the only ones I had any desire to impress. Bureaucrats and government officials? Not so much.

Yes. I had a ton of research and work to do. But I know my limits. Right then, my body was telling me I'd better be planning on giving it a few more hours of sleep very soon. I heeded warnings like that whenever possible.

My body and mind didn't just issue them willy-nilly. They meant it.

My plan was to show up at the office (after dropping by my house to shower and change clothes, of course) for an hour or so to check in with the team. Do the minimum amount of paperwork possible. And then head back home and to bed.

Unfortunately for me, those plans changed when I saw Steve Brighton sitting in his car outside the sheriff's station. It was pretty obvious at this time of night, that the man was just there waiting for me.

I parked in my reserved spot, and he met me halfway to the door to the station.

"Hey, Patty."

"Hey, Brighton. What's up?"

He smiled at me. "Nothing much. Just wanted to check in on the whole wolf case and maybe cash in that rain check for your celebratory dinner."

My eyes narrowed at the word wolf. To my mind, it hadn't been established as a wolf case yet. I was still trying to spin it to a large dog, dang it all. To that end, I didn't meet his eyes.

"It hasn't been determined there was a wolf involved," I told him. "You realize wolves don't just go around attacking people unprovoked, right?"

I didn't like his hesitation. "That's kind of what I wanted to talk with you about. If you have time." More hesitation as we reached the door. "In private."

I swallowed. That sounded serious. Not to mention awkward if I got the subtle hint about the conversation he wanted to have with me.

But what could I say? No? In a way, this was a conversation long overdue. I had just hoped to be in a much better place going into it. With a lot more sleep behind me, too.

Putting my hand on the doorknob, I stopped. "I have to do a quick check-in first. Then, sure, if you want to, we can meet to grab a bite to eat."

His shoulders fell a bit. "Good. I think this is important for you to know." Then he lowered his head and kissed me full on the lips. "I don't want you getting hurt because I didn't share needed information."

Before I could respond, he turned and walked back to his car. All I could do was just stand there and stare out after the man.

Well, this put a new spin on things. At least for me.

How on earth did a werewolf handle things when it would appear an agent of the infamous Luparri had their best interests at heart?

Goddess, but I was wishing I had time for a nap before that conversation. This was going to be… tricky.

Chapter 8

It didn't take me long to do what absolutely had to be done. Part of that was the simple reason that I really, really wanted to get that dreaded conversation over with.

The bad thing was, I knew I was going into it while not at my personal best. I also knew that when dealing with the Luparri, that wasn't a very smart, or safe, thing to do. Precautions needed to be taken.

So, I called Trevor. If anyone had a right to know, he did. After all, if this meeting went badly, as I greatly feared it might, then he might just be the one in the hot seat to figure out what the heck happened. A little forewarning seemed in order.

Just in case, mind you.

And yes, for the record, he tried to talk me out of it, or at the very least to let him be in on the meeting. While I appreciated the sentiments, that wasn't going to happen. I thanked him all the same.

Then I hung up and texted Steve. Instead of

texting me back, my phone immediately rang.

"Sorry," he said. "I figured this would be faster than texting back and forth."

The tension in his voice didn't do a dang thing to calm my nerves. I took a deep breath. "So, where are we meeting?"

"How about that little park close to your place?"

I frowned. "I thought there was food involved." My stomach rumbled. Yeah, it was definitely a sticking point. I might be willing to have this conversation with a lack of sleep, but not a lack of food. Wolves could be funny about that kind of thing. We got rather, well, testy when we were hungry.

He chuckled. "There is, I promise. I called in an order to Clucky's Palace. All I have to do is swing by and pick it up and then drive to meet you at the park."

I would have asked why we weren't just eating there, but I kind of thought I already knew the answer to that one. They wouldn't be all that busy at this time of night, but it was a pretty open space. Likely, the conversation we were about to have wouldn't be one either of us would want to be overheard.

"Sounds good. Do I need to bring anything?"

"Nope, I've got it covered. See you in twenty minutes?"

I agreed and hung up. Like it or not, this was

going to happen.

***

I don't know how he did it, but Steve beat me there. Probably because I took the time to say goodnight to all my workers and check in with the outside team one last time. Sue me, but I didn't want to be knee-deep in the upcoming talk and get a call.

That could still happen, of course, but I'd done everything I could to try to prevent it.

For the record, I was still wavering on how to handle this. If Steve spilled the wolfy beans, what was I going to do? Pretend it was all news to me? Let him know I already knew? Or, Goddess help me, tell him I was a werewolf myself?

The really scary thing was that I was leaning toward the latter. I only hoped that wasn't a sleep-deprived mind making a very bad decision.

I walked over to the quilt he had spread out in the center of the large clearing, my eyes fixating for a second or two on all that glorious meat. Steve knew my appetite, and the man hadn't skimped.

My eyes went from the food to his gaze. Why drag this unpleasantness out for possibly hours? That wasn't the kind of wolf I was. Better to pull that band-aid off quick, right?

"You're an agent of the Luparri, aren't you?"

His eyes widened, and he sucked in a breath.

"You really don't believe in dancing around the subject, do you?"

I shook my head. "Why do that? I really think we've danced long enough, haven't we?"

Steve hesitated, then nodded. "Now that you mention it, I guess we have at that." His eyes never wavered from mine. "Of course, your question pretty much answers mine."

I took a deep breath and nodded, trying my dangdest to be ready for anything that might happen next, up to and including the man going for a gun.

"I'm a Benandanti werewolf."

Well, he didn't go for his gun. That was something. But he did tense up. Big time.

Of course, I couldn't really blame him for that, now could I? Not with how tense I was at the moment.

When a full minute passed without either of us going for the other's throat, a little of the tension faded. Enough so that the heavenly aroma of the chicken laid out before us got a portion of my attention again.

"How's about we agree to a short truce while we eat?" I asked, not willing to give my full attention to the food until I had his word. Even then, probably not my full span. Some people didn't honor their word, and the Luparri didn't have that great of a reputation in the circle of werewolves.

For a very just cause.

He blinked at me, then gave a low chuckle.

"Deal."

We settled in and for the next ten minutes didn't say a word. It simply wasn't polite to talk with one's mouth full of glorious meat.

Finally, with my appetite almost abated, I swallowed and looked him in the eye. "You didn't seem all that surprised by my little announcement."

Steve shook his head. "I've known for a while now." Another low chuckle. "Didn't know you had me pegged as Luparri, though. Guess we were both on the same page, even if we didn't know it."

I took a slow drink from my soda, trying to get a read on him. Normally, I was good at reading people. Unfortunately, he seemed to be just as good at being a closed book.

"Where does this leave us? Do I have to fear for my life now? You going to try to turn me in to your superiors?"

He leaned back, and in what I could only describe as an extreme show of trust, he looked up to the moon above us. That movement spoke volumes. But he still hadn't given me a definite answer.

I waited. It was far too important of a question not to be answered.

"No. I don't think that's on the table right now."

Okay, I liked the first part of that statement, but I didn't much care for how he ended it. 'Right now' wasn't all that promising.

"And in the future?"

He shrugged. "As long as you don't go rogue wolf on me, you're safe. From me, at least." Then he turned back to me briefly. "That said, I think you and I both know we have a minor crisis right now."

Steve wasn't wrong, but I wasn't quite willing to go there yet. I rather thought we should iron things out between us first.

"I'm sorry if this hurts your feelings or anything, but I'm going to need more to go on. The Luparri doesn't have a reputation for working well with wolves. In fact, their reputation goes quite in the opposite direction. How do I know I can trust you?"

He shrugged, still making the effort to not meet my eyes. That had to be costing him something. "Same way I know I can trust you, I guess. We are at a bit of an impasse here, you know. Both of us are treading on uncharted grounds."

Steve hesitated, then finally glanced over at me. "As it turns out, we actually aren't the first to be in this particular situation. When I first found out you were a wolf—and don't ask, please, that's a story I'm not willing to share—I was really torn. I mean, I liked you. It threw me into a big moral dilemma. Then I remembered Jedadiah Crow."

"Jedadiah Crow?"

He nodded. "Yup. The two of us trained together in the Luparri, and Jed was one of the best of the best. Then, supposedly, he was bewitched by a werewolf, and the man up and retired."

I arched an eyebrow. "He did, did he?"

"He did. So I looked him up... and met the bewitching werewolf he's currently married to, too. Outstanding woman. She and her, well rather unusual, pack helped me see that maybe what the Luparri was teaching wasn't all fact. There are good werewolves as well as bad."

I grunted. "Duh. There are rotten apples in every barrel."

Steve's smile was a little on the crooked side. It was one of the small things I loved so much about him.

Wait a minute—did I just say loved?

I took a long look at him, and my heartbeat sped up. Double crap on toast. I did.

I'd been dancing around my feelings for the man because I knew—or at least had highly suspected—that he was a Luparri agent. But now that was all out in the open? Yeah, the feelings hit me hard.

I loved Steve Brighton. And dang, but that was going to complicate things.

Chapter 9

I stared at him for a long minute, trying to figure out how to ask what I needed to know. Finally, I just blurted it out. "You're still a Luparri agent, though, aren't you? If you know what they are… why?"

He plucked a long blade of grass and chewed on the end for a few seconds. Guess I wasn't the only one having to gather my thoughts before speaking right now.

When he finally spoke, he turned to look me directly in the eye. "It's kind of like that old adage. Keep your friends close and your enemies closer. Not that the Luparri are my enemies. Not yet, anyway. There are still some really good ones there. And who knows, maybe if we could gather strength in numbers, we could get the upper tier to see reason, too." He looked thoughtful. "That might be worth a shot in the future. And something that would be much easier done from inside than out."

"But you're taking their money, right? How does that work?"

He shrugged. "I have absolutely no moral dilemma about that. For now, I'm still doing exactly what they trained me to do. I'm still tracking rogue werewolves and bringing them to justice by whatever means necessary. That hasn't really changed. It's just that now I see not all werewolves are killer rogues."

I grunted. "You got that right. I'd say you might get one rogue in a thousand, if that. They are few and very far between."

Steve nodded slowly. "I'm beginning to think you're right." That crooked smile again. "Especially if you are any indication of what normal is for a werewolf."

I laughed. "Oh, that's funny. Me? Normal? No. Not by half." Not with half my blood being of the witchy variety. "But weres are still good, law-abiding citizens. We just happen to be fond of running in fur coats."

He laid back, his eyes going to the moon above us, and sighed. "I know I'm not supposed to feel this way, but I've always envied that about you all. The ability to get that close to raw nature itself." There was a pause. "You know those old werewolf movies? Any truth at all to them?"

I flopped on my back beside him. "If you're asking me if I can turn you into one of us, the answer is no. It doesn't work that way, I'm afraid. You're either born to it, or you aren't."

"I kind of thought that might be the case."

We laid in silence for a few minutes and the long day started taking its toll on my tired body. My mind started to drift off.

I blame that drifting off for what happened next.

"You know I'm going to have to investigate the death of Vinnie George, don't you?" he asked.

All I could do was sigh. "Yeah. You're taking money from the evil Luparri. You have to satisfy yourself that you aren't dealing with a werewolf killing. I get that." I paused. "But you also need to consider that if—and this is a very big if mind you—it really was a werewolf that killed George, it very well might have been in self-defense. What happens to your morals if that is the case?"

I didn't much like the silence that followed that question.

"I think I'm going to have to put the answer to that question on hold until I have more details on the matter. It depends on the circumstances that made a self-defense killing necessary. It's just not something I can give a blanket answer to without all the facts in place."

As much as I hated it, I could understand that.

"So," he said softly. "We working on this together or what?"

Again, I totally blame the drifting off part of

my brain, but that's how a Benandanti werewolf got teamed up to work with an agent of the evil Luparri.

Goddess, help me.

***

We parted ways shortly after that. I went home to my quiet little cabin and to bed for a much-needed few hours' sleep. And yes, I went to that bed alone. I was far too tired to be thinking of fun and games at this point.

It would have been much nicer, and more restful, if I could have gotten my brain to stop coming up with all the possible ways my little agreement with Steve could go wrong. There wasn't any shortage of ideas on that.

And no, my brain didn't stop even when it finally drifted off to what could most likely be called sleep. Or at least a reasonable facsimile of it.

As a witch, I had ways to deal with some of the likely scenarios that had cropped up. The main one, of course, was the one where I was being played by the Luparri to gain a roster of my pack members so they could take them out one by one at their convenience. That was the scenario that I hated the worst. For obvious reasons.

Again, I am a witch. I could handle that. Sort of.

The problem was that the method of handling

it wasn't exactly white magic. In order to safeguard my pack, I'd have to deal with magic that wasn't sparklingly pure. I'd also have to put myself at risk of being brought before the witches' council for a transgression of one of our primary rules.

You don't mess with a person's free will. It's as simple as that. That's why no witch in good standing with the council would ever touch a love spell with a ten-foot pole. It just wasn't worth the risk.

This, however, was different. We weren't talking teenage crush here. We were talking about the safety and protection of my fellow pack mates. If I was going to be working with a member of the Luparri on this, I'd dang well be taking precautions.

Besides, as long as Steve agreed with my precautions, the magic wouldn't be considered black. I wouldn't be working against his will if he agreed beforehand. That was important.

And if he didn't agree? Well, then the deal was off. It was just as simple as that.

To say that Steve was surprised to see me at his front door at five o'clock in the morning would be an understatement. He stood blinking at me from the doorway. "Patty? Has something happened?"

From the look of him, the man hadn't had the same problems I'd had with sleep. His adorably tussled hair and innocent, caring expression were enough to make me second guess what I was about to ask of him.

But then I wasn't just asking for myself. It wasn't my life I was playing with. He already knew about me. I wondered if that meant the Luparri did too. As I was still on this side of the earth and breathing, I would have to guess the answer to that one was no. He hadn't told them. Yet.

Unless, of course, this was all an elaborate plan to get my pack's member roster, and I was just the unwitting bait.

"Can I come in? We need to talk."

Steve sucked in a breath and nodded. "Those are four words no man ever likes to hear, but sure. Come in." He glanced at me, then into the kitchen of his small townhouse apartment. "Can I take the time to fix myself a cup of coffee? For some reason, I think I'm going to need it."

"Could you make that two cups?"

He nodded and shuffled off toward the kitchen. I'll admit to getting more than a little enjoyment from the view of that. It would have been a lot greater had the situation been different. Steve looked mighty fine, wearing nothing more than a pair of flannel pajama bottoms.

A lot of women went in for the chiseled abs look on a man. Not that Steve didn't have them, because he did. But I was more of an arm woman. Some women went for abs, some for the smile. I went for arms. I didn't like weak and scrawny or thick and dimpled. Wasn't much of a fan of the overly muscular weight-lifter look, either.

Steve's arms? Well, they were as perfect as the day was long. Just the right blend of athletic, muscular tone.

"Um, Patty? You okay?"

I glanced up from his arms to his face. That wasn't such a bad view, either. He was back standing before me, holding a cup of coffee out to me. I took it but didn't drink. I hadn't had him make it for me.

"Yeah, I'm fine." I carried the cup over to his tiny kitchen counter and sat down on one of his tall bar stools there. After a few seconds, Steve mirrored my movements.

"So, we need to talk?"

I nodded. "Yeah." I took a deep breath. "You're an agent of the Luparri, and if we are going to work together on an investigation, that is going to bring you into contact with a lot of werewolves." My eyes flashed to his. "Not that I'm saying I think a werewolf is our killer, mind you, but I'd be a fool to discount that possibility. Considering who the victim in question was."

"You're no fool," Steve said quietly. "But I think I'm starting to see your problem. You don't trust me not to betray your pack."

"I can't afford to rely on trust, Steve. Maybe if it was just me... but it isn't. I hope you understand that."

He didn't look happy, but he nodded. "I'd

probably do the same if I were you. I won't hold it against you."

I frowned at him. "That's not saying that I'm not willing to work with you. I'm saying that if we work together, you will have to agree to a... certain precaution on my part."

Now he was the one frowning. "Precaution?"

"Yup, precaution. First, I should ask, just to clear the air and all... You don't plan to turn my pack in to the Luparri, do you?"

"Not unless one of them turns out to be the killer, and the killing turns out to be questionable as to self-defense. You realize if that is the case, they will have to be dealt with, right?"

I arched an eyebrow at him. "I do. And as sheriff of Wind's Crossing, I'll be the one doing the dealing. Is that going to be a problem?"

I didn't much like the fact that he hesitated. Or the fact that he didn't come out with a straight answer, either.

"Can't we just work together to find the killer first, and then argue about who gets to take it from there?"

We stared at each other for a few minutes. In the end, I was the one who blinked. "Okay. I don't like it, but okay. But back to that precaution I was talking about... I'm not just a werewolf, I'm also a witch. And I've cooked up a little potion that will give me peace of mind that you'll keep your word about not turning in my pack mates to the Luparri."

He laughed and slapped the counter in front of us, making me jump. "Oh, Patty, you're a hoot. You really had me going there for a minute."

I just stared at him. "This isn't a joke, Steve. If you don't agree to take the potion, the deal is off. I can't work with you."

"Witches? Potions? Come on, what's the punchline?"

I blinked at him. "Let me get this straight. You know werewolves exist, and you don't believe witches have the power to do spells and potions?"

He shook his head at me. "Of course they do, but they aren't going to work. Not unless the person they're giving it to believes in that sh..tuff."

This could work in my favor. Who was I to argue? I took the vial of potion from my pocket and poured it into the quickly cooling cup of coffee before me, then pushed it over to him. "Then you won't have any problem drinking this. But you should know that this potion will not allow you to pass along any werewolf secrets to the Luparri. In any manner. Written, verbal, or sign language."

He stared at me, then down at the cup. "What's in it?"

I grinned at him. "If I was going to kill you, I'd just shoot you, you know. I have a gun."

"Ballistics ring a bell?"

Now I was the one laughing. "You think

they'd find your body, do you?"

"Touché." He hesitated only a second longer, then picked up the cup and raised it slightly to me. "To working together."

Then he drained the cup and handed it back to me. I reached over and placed a single finger on his forehead. "So mote it be."

A funny look crossed over his face. Well, it was funny to me. Probably not so much to him. The spell wouldn't be painful, but by now, he probably realized it was an actual thing and not some witch's pipe dream.

I'd done the right thing. I'd told him what the potion would do before I'd asked him to drink it, and he'd drank it willingly.

My witch's heinie was covered on this one, dang it all.

Chapter 10

This investigation was definitely becoming a group project. As a sheriff, I should be used to working in a group.

But I hadn't been a sheriff for all that long. We're talking days here. Before that, I was a solo operator.

This was going to take some getting used to. Throwing a Luparri agent into the mix of an already volatile situation might not have been the smartest move I'd ever made.

But then, what choice had I had? Word on the street was that being a part of the Luparri Initiative granted you the power to hide your scent. To a wolf, that ability is huge. That's how we know someone is nearby if they are trying to track us. Our super sniffers will alert us to the danger far before our eyes will.

It's a wolf thing.

Being tracked by someone that had no scent? Yeah, that's what made the Luparri such a deadly enemy to have. They had an unfair advantage. They were super sneaky.

If I hadn't let him onto the case, he would simply have tailed me. And I wouldn't have known it, and even more of the pack's secrets might have gotten out.

This way was better. Now, no matter how many secrets he learned, he couldn't pass them along to the Luparri. I'd just have to settle for that.

Even with all that in mind, I wasn't so sure about leading him straight to the pack's alpha wolves. If the Luparri information ever came out, and I'd taken him to visit the Nichols? Yeah. My furry hide wouldn't last long.

The bad thing was that Celia Nichols was one of two pack members with no alibi for the time frame of George's murder. To add even more bad to that, I couldn't just set Trevor to investigate that whole situation, because she'd want a reason why she was being treated as a suspect.

The penalties for letting a normal human in on the Benandanti secret were pretty severe. Again, knowing Celia, that alone would put my hide in danger.

That left Gray. I made the call, and he agreed to pick up the slack there. He might not have a background in law enforcement, but the man was smart as a whip. Not to mention an alpha wolf of his own pack. Those things meant something.

What meant even more was that I trusted him. Living the life I'd lived, and being through what I'd been through? I didn't trust a whole heck of a lot of people. Trust in the wrong person can get you killed in my line of work.

That left tracking down Donnie and Nell Adams and checking out the last wolf without an alibi. I glanced down at my notes from the joint pack meeting. That wolf had been from Gray's pack. But at least they weren't an alpha. That helped.

Tracking a pair of missing wolves who didn't have a very large, if any, footprint on the world wide web would not be easy. Nor was it likely to be a fast affair. Better to get Trevor started on that one. The big plus to that was that I was fairly sure that he'd have outside help on it. His mate, Amie, was an outstanding witch in her own right. That fact alone would make her an excellent partner for him. The fortunate coincidence that she was also a private investigator kind of sealed the deal.

Putting Trevor after Donnie and Nell was kind of like putting a small, and highly efficient, team on it. It felt right.

Which left me and Steve with the last non-alibied wolf. Gavin Mills seemed to be a pretty ordinary guy on the outside of things.

Then again, looks could be deceiving, couldn't they?

***

I had Gavin Mills' address and phone number that I'd collected at that joint pack meeting. I had that information for every wolf in a twenty-five-mile radius from Wind's Crossing. When I had a spare moment or two… all right, more like half a day… I'd be making a database with that information.

It was silly we didn't already have one, but then again, maybe we did, and I just hadn't run across it. Putting a list of known werewolves up on the internet really wasn't such a smart idea. There were hackers there.

I'd be keeping my database just for me, I thought. Still, it would be nice to have. Might even try to branch out for the other Benandanti creatures. Who knew when one of them might come in handy?

Unfortunately, an address and a phone number didn't really tell me all that much about the man. Other than the fact that he lived in the nicer part of Bear's Creek. Truthfully, that didn't say much more than his house probably came without wheels.

Not that there was anything wrong with living in a home on wheels, mind you. Gray had lived in one before hooking up with his new mate. No judging here. Mobility could be a good thing from time to time.

All this was a long-winded way to say that I needed to make a phone call before we headed out. To

Gray. I liked going into an interview with a little knowledge under my belt whenever possible.

He answered on the first ring. "Gray here."

"Hey, Gray. Patty. I'm getting ready to go pay a visit to Gavin Mills, and I was wondering if you had anything you thought I might should know first."

There was a brief silence.

"I wish I did. Gavin is a bit of an unknown up in Bear's Creek. He moved into town about five years ago. As far as I can tell, no one knows exactly what the man does for a living. Or if he does anything at all. He does have a website, if that helps." There was a pause, then he came back to the phone. "Gavin Mills, Inc. Has a dot com and everything. But the last time I checked, it really told little about him. Just that he's a consultant of some type. No actual details of any kind."

"Sounds like I've got my work cut out for me, then."

He laughed. "You and me both. You know it will not thrill Celia to see me at her door, right?"

Boy, did I ever. "You might want to make sure that her other half is there the first time you meet. At least Damon respects what it means to be an alpha. He'll keep her in check." And I'd be calling the man to let him know Gray was working with me, too. That should lend him a little weight.

"Hope you're right. I'll let you know how it goes." He paused. "I'd like it if you'd do the same."

"Goes without saying, Gray. Stay safe."

"You too."

We hung up, and I took a very deep breath. It was time to call Steve and get this show on the road.

Goddess and Creator help me. I had a bad feeling I was going to need both of them at my back for this one.

Chapter 11

The house didn't look evil. That was good. In fact, it was quite a respectable house. Nothing too fancy, but nothing shabby or in ill repair either.

Hopefully, that spoke well for the man inside. But we'd soon find that out for ourselves.

Steve wasn't too happy about me taking the lead. That was his problem, not mine. I was the one with the sheriff's badge, dang it all. As it was that badge that opened the door for us, I was the one in charge. He'd just have to deal with his issues of inferiority, or whatever they were, on his own time.

It took a full minute and three times knocking before the door slowly opened. I could have been wrong, but I really thought if I hadn't been in full uniform, that still wouldn't have happened. But it did.

I nodded to the man behind the chain. "Gavin Mills?"

He nodded back. "That's me." He hesitated. "Can I ask what this is about?"

Here is where having Steve along proved problematic. What I really wanted to do was mention the pack and the fact that I had Gray's approval to be here. As one of Gray's pack members, that would mean something. But the man at my back stopped that cold. Anyone with half a nose would know he wasn't a wolf.

"Vinnie George," I said, watching his eyes. They never blinked. "I need to talk with you about your whereabouts during the time of his murder."

The man didn't move to unlatch the chain. Instead, he just blew out a long breath. "I've already told you my whereabouts. I was home alone that whole day, evening, and night. It wasn't me." And the door started to shut. Right up until it hit the reinforced toe of my boot.

"I still want a conversation. Your choice as to whether that takes place here or down at the station." When he still didn't remove the chain, I added. "I really don't think that chain would hold up against me, do you?" It probably helped that I put a little magic behind the words. No sense dragging this thing out for any longer than we had to.

His eyes widened, but the chain came off and the door opened wider. Gavin looked from me to Steve and back again. "Not so sure I want him to come in."

"Sorry. He's with me. It's non-negotiable."

Gavin hesitated again, but when he saw I

wasn't about to back down, he stepped to one side and let us in. The living room we stepped into was every bit as ordinary as the outside of the house had been. I was sensing a theme here.

Just an ordinary Joe lives here. Nothing to see, move along. And yes, it was making me think just the opposite was the truth of things.

We all sat down, and Gavin looked at me. "I don't know what else I can tell you. If I'd known the man was going to be killed, I'd have made sure to have an alibi available. But I didn't, so I don't. Not much I can do about that now."

I smiled at him. "No, there isn't. And I appreciate the upfront honesty about that fact, too. It doesn't make my job any easier when people lie about that."

He blinked at me. My smile must have caught him off guard. Good. That's what I'd been hoping for.

"Did you know Vinnie George?"

Gavin looked down at his hands resting on his knees. It took a minute, but finally, he answered. "You don't know how bad I want to say no, but I think you and I both know I can't say that truthfully." He glanced pointedly at Steve and sniffed. "People like me and you, Sheriff, know people like Vinnie George."

I nodded. "That we do. But I'd be interested in some details on just how you knew him."

Gavin sighed and leaned back in his chair.

"Not well. And no, we didn't exactly get along. He was stalking and harassing a client of mine, and I... made him stop. He wasn't a big fan of mine after that."

"What exactly do you do for your clients, Mr. Mills?" Steve asked.

I frowned at him. So much for him getting the message this was my show. Unfortunately, his eyes were firmly on Gavin, so he missed my rebuke, small as it had been.

"Usually, I help them with bad PR. But I have been known to help people fix other situations they find themselves in, too."

"What kinds of situations? And exactly how do you help them fix it?" Steve asked.

He shrugged. "I do what it takes." Then he caught a look at my face. "Within the law, I assure you."

The throbbing pulse at the base of his throat had me thinking just maybe that wasn't as true as he said it was. "And the client that you helped with Vinnie George? What was that about?"

Gavin swallowed but shook his head. "I'm sorry. I truly am, but I can't talk about that. My service is based on trust and confidentiality. I can't tell you who my client was or the nature of the case. I hope you understand that."

"You can leave the client's name out of it," I said. "For now, anyway. But I have to insist that you tell me your dealings with Vinnie George. This is a murder investigation. That trumps confidentiality clauses."

"I was afraid you'd think that." He looked away.

I gave him a minute. I owed him that, I thought. So far, the man had been more open to answering questions than I'd expected.

Gavin finally turned back to me. "It wasn't much of a big deal, I don't think. But you might feel differently. Vinnie was harassing my client, but he was keeping to the letter of the law and there wasn't anything the person could do to stop it. So I did some digging on Vinnie George and came up with a little tidbit from his past." His eyes left mine again.

I got the message pretty clearly. "You blackmailed Vinnie George, didn't you?"

He nodded. "Yes. I did. But I sure as heck didn't kill him."

A shiver crossed my spine as I plainly heard the unspoken next words. "I didn't need to." Something told me that the man in front of me would do anything for a client if the pay was good enough. And I really didn't think in my heart that his hands were totally free of blood.

Unfortunately, I also believed that blood didn't come from Vinnie George. I really didn't think Gavin Mills was our killer.

This time.

Just as I reached that ultimate conclusion... and before I had a chance to ask the obvious follow-up questions... my cell phone rang. I pulled it from my pocket and glanced at it. Trevor.

I stood and waved the phone. "I have to take this. Excuse me for a minute." I crossed the room to stand by the front door. What I really wanted to do was step out onto the porch, but it probably wasn't such a great idea to leave a Luparri alone in the room with a Benandanti werewolf unsupervised. Especially as Steve would likely have come to the same conclusion as I had about the cleanliness of the man's history.

"Patty here. What you got?"

"Well, I just heard from the coroner, and you're gonna love this." He paused for a few seconds, but when I didn't respond, he went on. "Vinnie George isn't Vinnie George."

"Come again?"

Trevor chuckled. "Yeah, that was pretty much what I said to the coroner, too. Turns out the man's real name is George Vincent. He probably changed it up to keep the outstanding warrants on him from three separate states being served."

I turned toward the door and lowered my voice. "He was wanted in three states?"

"Yup. Indiana warrants are for impersonating a police officer and intimidation. Ohio wants him for reckless discharge of an unpermitted and undisclosed firearm on public property. And Illinois wants the man for a series of domestic battery charges. Apparently, George's only vice wasn't wolf-hunting."

"It would definitely appear that is the case, yes." I glanced back into the living room. Gavin Mills was staring directly at me, a smug look on his face. I had a feeling he knew all too well what the call was all about.

"See if you can get those states to forward those files to us. Maybe we'll get lucky and there will be something in one of them to wrap this up."

Another chuckle. "Great minds, Patty. Already put the request in. We should have them in a couple of hours."

"Good. I appreciate you letting me know." I did, too. It was always better to know information like this instead of having to ferret it out of people like Gavin. A heck of a lot more trustworthy source, too.

We hung up, and I went back to join the men. The smug look was still firmly on Gavin's face. I wanted desperately to smack it off there, but I had that stupid badge to think about, so I didn't.

"Let me guess," Gavin said, upping his smirk. "Surprising news from the coroner's office?"

I just looked at him until he started to squirm. I might not have my own pack, but I was still a bloody alpha wolf, and it was about time the man started treating me with a bit of respect. It took a minute, but eventually, he got the message.

Only then did I answer him. "You could say that. I'm going to need everything you have on George Vincent. All the dirt you dug up. And I do mean all of it. If you hold out on me, I won't hesitate to press charges against you for obstructing a legal investigation. Are we clear?"

He swallowed. "As a bell. Give me a couple of minutes." He stood, and I followed him, stepping right up to him and taking a big sniff. He swallowed again. Good, he got my meaning.

If the man had any intentions of running, he knew I had his scent now.

And that meant that no matter how far the man ran, I'd bloody well Find him.

As a wolf or as a witch, it really didn't matter.

Chapter 12

Technically, this wasn't a joint investigation. The case had zilch to do with his jurisdiction (other than the Luparri thing), and we both knew that. So would the rest of my team.

So Steve went to pull his shift with his department, and I went back to my office to check in with Trevor. He was waiting for me at the door with coffee.

If only all my deputies were that good. Some were close. Others, well, there were a few holdouts that really didn't enjoy answering to a woman, sheriff's badge or no. Those were a work in progress. They'd adapt, or they'd be gone.

I was really only waiting to see if I was going to last through this probation thing. No sense mixing things up if I wasn't going to be there long.

"How are you coming with finding the runners?" I asked him.

He took a sip from his cup before answering.

"Good news and bad news on that end."

I raised an eyebrow and waited. What was it with men and holding out information? It didn't take him long to get the message.

"We found Donnie Adams' old pickup truck. That's the good news…"

"Don't even think about stopping there. Just get it all out, all right?"

He grinned at me. "The bad news is where we found it. On an access road near the South Branch of AuSable."

Crapsnackles. He hadn't been kidding about that bad news part, had he?

Trevor glanced around, but it was just the two of us there by the front door. Probably why he had met me there. For privacy.

He still lowered his voice. "There are over three thousand acres in that preserve area. Are you thinking they went to ground? As… you know?"

Even with no one around, there was always the possibility of being overheard. I was thankful he was taking precautions. I ran a hand through my hair and nodded.

"Yeah. That's what I'm thinking, all right. According to Gray, Donnie and Nell were big into the outdoors. They know how to live off the land. With the river for fish and water, and the small game in the forest? They could last a very long time up there."

He looked thoughtful. "Can't be comfortable

camping out right now, though. It still gets pretty cold at night."

I just looked at him.

"Ah, yes. So, not really an issue, is it?"

"Not really, no. In the dead of winter, maybe it would be, but in May… not so much. A good sleeping bag and they'd be warm and comfy."

He seemed surprised by my words. Most likely he'd thought they'd have their fur to keep them warm, but that wasn't the case when a Benandanti slept. When we slept, we always went to skin form. Whether we wanted to or not. A hard body reboot, as it were.

"We get those files on George yet?"

"They were coming over the fax as I came out here to meet you. Should be finished printing by now."

We walked into the bustling office, and I stopped by the fax machine to collect the papers. Then the two of us headed to my office. We left the door open.

This part of the investigation was open to other ears. Nothing to hide. I really hoped it was this part that panned out to lead to the killer.

It would be so much simpler that way.

"I'm thinking we can rule out the domestic battery case," Trevor said. "George's ex-wife was a Latino. After the divorce, she moved back to Mexico. Guess her new life here in America didn't really pan out to be better for her."

"Not married to a man like that, it wouldn't. Any family still up here?"

He shook his head.

"Well, that's one we can put on the back burner, then." I took one stack of papers, and he took the other.

I ended up with the one from Indiana. Impersonating a police officer and intimidation. It made for very interesting reading.

George Vincent had stolen a deputy sheriff's uniform and had worn it to try to muscle a post office worker into letting him confiscate his ex-wife's outgoing mail. It hadn't worked so well for him.

I didn't like the fact that it once again tied in with the ex-wife, but it still wasn't enough for me to take that case off the back burner. I just wasn't feeling it.

But my witch's intuition kicked into high gear when I went further into the file and saw the name of the postal worker. James Allen.

"Trevor?"

"Yeah?"

"Didn't we recently get a new Post Master at the post office?"

He laid down the paper he'd been scanning to look at me. "We did. Jimmy Allen." He paused. "Don't tell me."

I shrugged. "Okay, I won't say a word then.

But I think maybe the two of us need to pay Jimmy a visit."

He was already grabbing his jacket. But then, so was I.

***

James Allen wasn't anything like what I expected. The man barely stood five and a half feet tall, if that, and weighed next to nothing. As in, a good strong wind could quite literally blow the man off his feet.

Not the kind of man I'd have expected to stand up to a bully like George. But he had. The man had stood his ground and called in the law rather than giving way to George. That showed guts and a fair amount of spunk.

Two qualities I liked to see in a person.

He looked up from his desk behind the counter when we walked in. His face got a little lighter as the blood drained from it, but he squared his shoulders and stood to greet us.

"I've rather been expecting you to show up. Can you give me a minute?"

I took a deep breath, gathering in the man's scent at the same time. Only then did I nod. I'd have told him to keep in sight, but we'd parked right beside the man's Jeep, and both vehicles were in plain view outside the big glass window of the small office.

It wouldn't take Trevor and me long to give chase if he made for the Jeep. And if he just flat out ran… well, the scent I'd just taken in would come in very handy, wouldn't it?

Lucky for him and us, running didn't appear to be in the man's plans.

He came back out from the side room with a lady who then sat at his desk. That made sense. He couldn't very well leave the front counter unmanned.

Then he stepped out from the metal security door at the side to meet us in the lobby. From there, we went to stand outside beside our cars. That part of it was his choice.

Can't say I blamed him, either. I wouldn't want to talk about this in front of a co-worker if I was him, either.

"If you were expecting us to show up, then I'm going to assume you know why we're here," I said. Yes, I was being vague for a reason. You learned things that way sometimes. This just happened to be one of those times.

James swallowed, but he still stood tall. Well, as tall as the man could. "Fran mentioned me, didn't she?"

My mind whirled. Fran? How did I know that name? It didn't take long for my brain to process that bit of information. Fran Michaels was the one who had found George Vincent's body.

Trevor was right there with me. "You want to

explain that?"

There was a reason Trevor was my right-hand deputy. He understood the being vague thing. It especially helped when you didn't have a clue what the suspect was talking about. Like now.

James took a couple of deep breaths. "I had hoped she didn't see me, but I must have been wrong about that, huh?"

Trevor and I just looked at him. There was a time for being vague, and there was a time for keeping your trap shut. This was a time for the latter.

Eventually, he got the hint. Silence tends to make suspects jumpy. I like it when they get jumpy. That's when tasty little morsels of truth come out.

"Look, I didn't kill the man, okay? No, I didn't like him. And yes, we had a past. But I didn't kill him."

Okay, so things were starting to come together a little more for me. Enough so that I took a chance. "So, why were you there?"

He looked away. "This is going to sound really bad, but I'm telling the total truth here, okay? You should know I would never lie to an officer of the law. It's not who I am."

"Truth generally wins out in the end. It's better to start off with it, I think," I said.

James nodded, but he didn't look thrilled at the idea of sharing. If he was at that crime scene when George got killed, I could understand that.

"As I've said, I don't like George. The man was scum. Worse than scum. I wanted him out of my town. If I'd known the man lived here, I never would have taken the position at the Post Office. Not with our past. But I didn't know, and I did."

"Still doesn't explain what you were doing there," Trevor prompted.

James grunted. "I'm getting to that. I'd heard that George had a habit of hunting that park. Illegally, I might add. Number one because it's a posted no-hunting zone, and number two because the man is a felon and can't legally carry a firearm in the state of Michigan."

He raised a hand to comb through his hair. "I've been following him to get shots of him. Once I built enough to prove my case, I was going to bring them to you. Then, this all happened, and I kind of thought those images might just make me look like your number one suspect, so I didn't."

"We'll be needing those pictures," I told him.

He pulled an SD card from his breast pocket and handed it to me. "They're all on this." He paused. "Including the ones I took the night George was killed."

I frowned at him. "Did George have a gun with him that night?" I mean, if he didn't, then why did he take the pictures?

"Yeah. There had been a wolf sighting in the park. I figured with George's reputation, he wouldn't be able to pass up the opportunity to add another wolf's hide to his collection."

Double crapsnackles. Not only did that turn the investigation back to a possible wolf as the killer, but it also added another minor mystery to the whole thing.

Because we hadn't found a gun with George's body.

Chapter 13

Trevor offered to put the SD card into his phone so we could take a look at the images right there in the car. But I didn't see much sense in that.

One, we were only a minute from the station, and two, we'd be able to see things a lot clearer on a bigger screen. I rather thought that the last one was kind of important.

The very first picture showed George Vincent getting out of his vehicle in the parking lot of the park. The date stamp was the night of the murder. And James hadn't been lying about the gun, either. Unless the man had something else stored in that rifle bag on his back, the man was definitely carrying a firearm.

A single image later and any doubt was gone. The gun was out and in George's hand.

I stared at it for a long minute. As much as I hated to admit it, I wasn't that up on the makes and models of firearms. I had to carry a pistol as part of the job, and I didn't much care even for that. I had other, much more satisfying ways, to defend myself.

"Can you make out what kind of rifle that is?" I asked Trevor.

He nodded. "Looks like a Remington Model Seven to me. It's a bolt action model. A lot of the heavy hunters in this area use them."

I reached for the phone on my desk and dialed the coroner's office. A few minutes later, I was pretty sure my theory would pan out. The bullet they dug out of George had come from a Remington Model Seven rifle.

As rifles weren't allowed on state or public property without ultra-special permission, which as a felon George would never get in a million years, the possibility of two of the exact model being on the scene that night was slim indeed.

It looked like George carrying that gun illegally had truly been the death of him. He'd been shot with his own weapon.

But how would a capable hunter like George have let that happen?

We pulled up the other images on the card kind of in a big collage on the screen. There were only six images, so after a quick glance at all of them together, we started going one by one with them. The hope was that once we enlarged the image on the screen, we'd see something of interest.

That happened when the fourth picture blew up onto the screen. I could tell that Trevor saw something, as he sucked in a quick breath and pointed at the screen.

"That looks like a trail cam."

My eyes followed his pointing finger. Even with him pointing the thing out, it was hard to find. I glanced up at him.

"How on earth did you see that so fast?"

He grinned and shrugged. "I've got a bit of a past when it comes to trail cams. That slight glow there is a dead give-away."

"All right then. Looks like it's time for another road trip."

I didn't have to tell him twice. He was already holding the door open for me.

***

When you are driving a marked sheriff's vehicle, you don't have to run with lights and sirens blaring to make good time. Within a matter of minutes, we were parked in the small lot and making our way toward the bend in the path that led straight to the crime scene.

That making good time thing was important to note, because if we'd been even a couple of minutes later, we'd have missed our golden opportunity. Not to mention the fact that the cam and any clues it might hold to the identity of the killer would have been gone, too.

But lucky for us—and not so lucky for the man hastily climbing down from the tree in question—we made it in time for the fun. The man took one glance back at us, gave a little chirp, and gathered himself to run. Trevor just laughed.

"Really, Billy? You think you can outrun me?"

The man stopped in his tracks, his shoulders dropping even as he turned back toward us. His Adam's apple was bobbing for all it was worth from all the hefty swallowing the man was doing as he took the few steps over to us. Slow steps, but at least he made them of his own free will.

Kind of, anyway.

"This isn't what it looks like," he said.

I threw a very pointed glance at the trail cam still attached to his wrist by a short, braided cord. "Oh?"

The swallowing continued. "I wasn't trying to hide evidence or anything like that," he said, rushing his words more than a little. "I swear if this holds anything that would help you figure out who killed Vinnie, I'd have gladly handed it over to you."

"Anonymously, of course," Trevor said.

The man blushed but nodded. "Well, yeah. This next part is going to be awkward for me."

I glanced at Trevor and then back at the man. My partner had an advantage over me here, as he knew the man. I didn't. So I raised an eyebrow and asked the obvious question, "The next part?"

The man wouldn't meet my eyes. His gaze went back to the trees as if he hoped something would come from them to stop things from progressing any further.

Nothing did.

"I believe he's referring to the part where we ask him why that trail cam was up there in the first place," Trevor said. "You see, Billy here is what you'd call an honest man. He'd never lie to the authorities, which means he's stuck with having to tell us the truth. No matter how awkward that truth might be." He paused. "Isn't that right, Billy?"

Billy nodded. For the record, he looked like he wished Trevor's words weren't true, but I had a feeling they were. My partner was an excellent judge of character. If he said Billy was an honest man, then you could take that to the bank.

"So, are you going to make us actually ask?" I asked.

Billy took a deep breath, then shook his head. "I guess not."

It wasn't only the man's face that was red now. The color went all the way into the man's hairline and down into his neck. For all I knew, the man's entire body was blushing. That's a whole lot of embarrassment right there.

"I was trying to figure out Fran's running schedule. She mixes it up a lot."

I frowned. That didn't sound so very innocent to me. In fact, it sounded more than a little creepy. "You are stalking Fran Michaels?"

He shuddered. "No! It's not like I have some kind of evil plan or anything. I just wanted to, well, accidentally run into her while she's jogging. You know, kind of a happy circumstance kind of thing." He paused for another deep breath. "I'm not so good when it comes to women."

If this was how he had decided to go about meeting Fran, I could well believe that. I looked over at Trevor, and he nodded.

"As I said, Billy wouldn't lie to us. Especially not with us being in uniform and everything."

I rubbed my chin, thinking. "Well, as far as I know, there's no law against setting up a trail cam to get pictures of… wildlife. And I'm sure you get a fair share of that, right?"

Billy gave an enthusiastic nod. "Oh, yeah. Some really good shots, too."

"All right then. I'm willing to forget that part about Fran if you hand that cam and the SD card over to us. We'll return it when we're finished going over everything." That return thing was important, as it did not appear to be a cheap affair. In fact, it looked quite state-of-the-art.

The man glanced from me to Trevor and back again. I could tell he still had something he wanted to say, but he didn't. He simply detached the cord from his wrist and handed everything over to me.

Trevor was a step ahead of me on this one. "I'm afraid that doesn't include the images on the cam, Billy. And I'd highly recommend you try to find another way to meet Fran that isn't quite so… stalkerish."

"Oh, I know her," Billy said, his shoulders dropping. "We go to the same church. I just can't summon up the courage to actually ask her out. I was hoping if we met on the trails a few times, maybe that would change."

"Let me get this straight," I said. "You and Fran already know each other, and you are both runners?"

He nodded miserably.

I just shook my head. Then I reached up and covered my sheriff's badge with one hand. This next part wasn't going to come from the sheriff part of me.

"I think you're missing an excellent opportunity to be her knight in shining armor here."

Billy just blinked at me. "I am?"

"Think about it. She found a dead body in the woods. The woods where she frequently runs. Don't you think she'd feel a little safer if she had a big, strong man to run with? There is safety in numbers, you know. You wouldn't even have to frame it as asking her out. Just offer to be her running buddy."

Trevor just grinned at me. "You know, that really could work. How's about it, Billy? Think you could handle that?"

From the sudden hope in the man's eyes, I thought just maybe the answer to that was yes.

Chapter 14

We let Billy go with a warning to tone his stalkerish ways down. I was relying a lot on Trevor's judgment of the man. My deputy hadn't let me down with his calls so far. I was really hoping this wouldn't be a first in that department.

It didn't take long to make it back to the station and back, once again, to our larger-screened monitor to review our newest picture hoard. There were a lot more images to go through this time.

Billy had set his camera to take only one shot when it detected movement in its field of vision. After that, the camera was set to wait at least ten minutes before taking another image. To his mind, that one shot was enough to see whether or not Fran was on the trail. And that one-shot deal helped to keep the memory on the SD card freed up for more images.

Unfortunately, that one shot wasn't nearly enough for us.

Especially once we got a good look at the

images taken the night of the murder. That took a while. Billy hadn't changed out the memory card for a few nights, so there were a lot of pictures to sort through before we struck gold.

But strike gold we did.

The bad news was that this gold strike was going to open a massive can of trouble. For me, and quite possibly the world at large.

Because right there on that screen I was staring at was a rather large wolf standing over George's body. I could tell Trevor was looking at me even before he spoke.

"Is there any way to tell if that's a werewolf or just the garden variety wolf?"

It was a good question. Normally, the answer to that question would be no. When we Benandanti change into our fur forms, there is no difference between us and a one hundred percent, non-shifting wolf. At least, not on the outside.

However, that wasn't the answer this time. That was true because I knew that wolf.

I should.

Because the wolf standing over the dead body of George Vincent was none other than the female alpha of my honorary pack. The wolf without the alibi.

Goddess, but this was bad.

If I'd been honoring my deal with Steve, I would have called him in immediately. But I didn't.

To be honest, I really didn't think bringing a Luparri agent in on the arrest of an alpha wolf would be such a great idea.

He'd either forgive me or he wouldn't. That would be up to him. Letting him know once I had the woman safely behind bars would be a much better option for me, I thought. Less risk of his taking over and deciding to do things the Luparri way, for one thing.

There was always that risk. I'd known that right from the beginning. And no. It wasn't a risk I much liked. My relationship with Steve Brighton might just be doomed before it actually bloomed into something lasting. Only time would tell on that.

I looked Trevor in the eyes. "You okay if I bring in Gray on the takedown? I think we could use a third person for backup, and I really think it would help if they knew the full score going into this." And that wasn't true of any of my staff other than Trevor.

He nodded. "No problem here." He paused. "In fact, you might want to make him a reserve deputy for things like this in the future. It might come in handy."

The man wasn't wrong.

***

I took the risk and waited until I knew Celia and Damon would both be home from work. Gray

106

hadn't had any luck getting to talk with Celia yet. He had taken my warning to heart about the wisdom of having Damon in on that first meeting. Knowing what I knew now, that was probably for the best.

It was my hope that Damon would be level-headed about this. Of course, I was fairly certain that wouldn't be the case with Celia. She wasn't exactly level-headed at the best of times. Power corrupts some wolves. Celia was one of them.

The thought of leaving Trevor out of the arrest crossed my mind, but not for long. With a non-werewolf on the premises, the alphas would have to think long and hard about shifting for a quick get-away. And I also liked the numbers of three against two.

The Nichols weren't alphas of an entire pack for nothing. They were strong. Very strong. And more than a bit ruthless, too.

Gray met us there, and we parked a block down from their house. Then we walked the rest of the way. I was going for as much of a surprise as I could muster. Part of me suspected Celia knew I'd be coming for her sooner or later, and that she'd most likely made contingency plans for just such an event.

I sent Gray around to the back of the house to cover the rear exit, and Trevor and I walked straight up to the front porch. After we'd given Gray enough time to get situated. That was important.

Unfortunately, I really didn't think Celia

coming with us of her own free will was in the cards. I knew the woman too well to expect that to happen. She'd fight, or she would run. I was kind of betting on the running thing.

But then, there were three of us and only one of her. Well, two if you counted her mate. Again, I was truly hoping Damon would be the least of our worries. That didn't mean I didn't have my taser at the ready.

Alpha or no, with all that electricity running through a person's body, they would go down. Whether they were wearing skin or fur really wouldn't make much of a difference, either.

Best of all, it wasn't a fatal solution. I liked that. Celia wasn't my favorite person, or wolf either, for that matter. That didn't mean I wanted the woman dead. Just in custody where I could ask her some good, hard questions.

Damon opened the door and stood there for a few seconds in silence. I was the one to finally break it.

"May we come in?"

He took a deep breath but stepped to one side to let us through. The main living room was empty. I glanced around, but there was no sign of Celia.

"Is your wife home?"

Damon blinked at me, then nodded. "She is."

He would not give me an inch here, would he?

"I need to talk to her."

His eyes traveled down my arm to where I had one hand resting on my taser. "Somehow, I don't think talking is all you have in mind here."

"That depends on how open she is to being truthful with me. I have proof that hasn't been the case thus far. So yes. I intend to take her in for questioning. The rest is up to her, and to what really happened to George Vincent."

Things could have gone from bad to worse at that point, but luckily, Damon was one to acknowledge the right way of doing things. And that was not to get in the way of me doing my dang job. He had to know that bucking me wouldn't have ended well.

I might not be the alpha of a pack, but I was still an alpha. And a witch to boot. That meant something, too. I was an oddity. And the wolves in the area knew better than to underestimate what I was capable of.

"Celia," Damon called out. "You need to come downstairs. The sheriff wants a word with you."

I grimaced. He just had to give her that little warning, didn't he?

It didn't surprise me when I heard her shout from above me and then, well, all heck broke loose.

I'd been in the Nichols' house before, and I knew that there was a back staircase. I was none too gentle pushing past Damon on my way to those steps' exit into the kitchen. Even so, I was too late.

The back door stood wide open, and Celia's frenzied scent went right through it. I just hoped Gray had been ready.

I ran through the door with Trevor on my heels. Then promptly tripped over the inert body of a naked woman. Crapsnackles. I picked myself up and looked around, but there was no sign of Gray.

I looked back at Trevor and pointed down at the woman. "Make sure she's okay and stay with her. If she comes to, don't let her leave." I was pretty sure the woman on the ground had been in fur form before Gray took her down.

I was also fairly certain that said werewolf had been part of Celia's contingency plan. But the missing Gray was a worry.

Trevor grunted, and I was about to take off after Celia's scent when I heard a car start up at the front of the house, gravel spinning as it took off out of the driveway.

Double crapsnackles. I had a funny feeling that Celia was in that car. But I couldn't leave without making sure Gray was all right. Besides, by the time I made it back to my patrol car, I'd have no way to know which way to go.

Scent really didn't work with cars involved.

That left me just one path to follow. I gathered Gray's scent and ran.

Chapter 15

The good news was double-fold. One, I didn't have all that far to run. Two, when the scent trail led me to Gray, he was on his feet and fine.

He was also dressed far differently than he had been the last time I saw him, which had only been a matter of minutes ago. Then, he had been wearing jeans and a snug-fitting tee-shirt. Now, those clothes were gone and all the man had on was a short pair of jogging shorts.

All that said, he was still wearing more clothes than the woman he was leading by the scuff of her neck. The bad news was that the woman he was leading wasn't Celia. A fact I could tell he was none too happy about.

His face flushed. "I'm sorry. They caught me by surprise, and all I caught was a glimpse of the back of this one running. She looks just like Celia from the back. Should have gone by scent." He grimaced. "Then I wouldn't have gotten the wrong runner."

I swallowed and nodded. He was right, but there was no sense in making the man feel bad. He wasn't used to dealing with the criminal element. I was. He'd gone on instinct, which, most likely, had been what they'd been counting on.

"Don't feel too bad. I have more than scent on my side to find her."

He brightened a little and gave me a slow smile. "That's right. You do." Then he paused. "I'd kind of like to be with you when you cast that spell."

"Count on it."

In a matter of minutes, we were back with Trevor, who was impatiently waiting with the first woman. She'd since come to and was desperately trying to talk him into letting her go. Right. Like that was going to happen.

I looked at the two women, neither of whom had yet to say a word in my presence. "Either of you got clothes nearby?"

They looked at each other, and finally, one of them broke and nodded. "There's a bag in the corner of Celia's kitchen."

Smart woman. She must have decided that going into a public jail naked as a jaybird wasn't the most prudent of options. And right now, I wasn't all that much leaning toward making their lives easier for them. But that could wait until we got them to the station.

Trevor retrieved the bag in question, then

quietly turned his head to allow the women a small amount of privacy to get dressed. If either of them tried anything, that privacy thing would disappear faster than you could blink. But they didn't make a move.

They had to know by now that they were well and truly in trouble. I mean, the two of them were members of the pack. As such, I knew them. Knew where each of them worked, too. Where did they have to run?

I just had one tiny little detail to take care of before getting them into the patrol car.

Walking back into the house, I found Damon standing at the kitchen table, his arms crossed tight against his chest. Our eyes met in a heated glare.

"She got away, didn't she?"

I nodded. "For now. She's only delayed the inevitable. I'm not just a wolf, you know."

He swallowed, then nodded. "True. Don't suppose you'd be willing to let the pack handle this?"

All that got was a shake of my head. "Sorry, Damon. This is murder we're talking about. That's way outside the realms of pack politics."

"I was afraid that's what you'd say." Then he paused. "So, you taking me in too?"

I raised an eyebrow. "Should I?" I mean, the man had a rock-solid alibi for the night of George's death. Then again, he had given Celia the warning she'd needed to escape custody. I could have brought him in for that alone. But at least he hadn't actively attacked me or either of my companions. For that, I was willing to cut him a bit of slack.

"I had nothing to do with George's death, if that's what you're asking."

"Then I think I can leave you out of this. For now. But if Celia contacts you, it would be wise to let me know that."

He nodded. I could tell he was agreeing to the truth of my words, not agreeing to follow through with my request. Too much more of that and the man would be in my custody.

"You two share a bathroom?"

Damon blinked at me. "What's that got to do with this?"

"I want to see the bathroom that Celia uses in the morning."

More blinking. I could tell he wanted to say no. Probably because by now he had guessed what it was I wanted... and more importantly, why I wanted it.

A few hairs from Celia's brush. Lucky for Damon, he knew I was at the end of my rope with him.

I left with the hair I needed.

***

Part of me wanted to cast that danged Find

spell on Celia immediately and bring her in. That part was saying that it was important to get hands on her before she got enough distance between us to create issues with jurisdictions and little things like that.

But the other part of me wanted answers first. And my witch's intuition was telling me that one or the other of the women in front of me could give me those answers. Or at the very least, a start to them.

Trevor and I ended up separating, each of us taking one of them. I thought it was important for us not to give them a chance to get their stories straight in the backseat on the way to the station. So I took Flora Johnson with me in Gray's car and left the patrol car to Trevor and Emma Rikes.

Of the two, I had hoped that Flora would be the easier to be intimidated into talking. A silent ride to the station with the sheriff might loosen her up a bit. That was my hope, anyway.

While Trevor was taking care of Emma—and the necessary paperwork for their detainment—I ushered Flora into an interview room. One with no two-way windows or tech listening options.

This would be a private little heart-to-heart. Wolf to wolf.

By the time we got settled at the small table, Flora was ready to break. I could tell it. I'd been doing this kind of work for a very long time. A lot longer than I'd been sheriff. All the signs were there.

If I could just manage not to blow it. With all

my experience, I'd still done that more times than I could shake a stick at. I didn't want this to be one of them.

So I just sat there and waited her out. Couldn't really mess things up if I said nothing, now could I? Well, okay, but at least the chances were drastically reduced.

It didn't take all that long.

"Celia didn't kill him." Her voice was quiet and had a bit of a tremble to it. "I wasn't covering for a murderer."

I mulled that over. There wasn't any doubt in her voice. Not one single ounce of it. She was telling the truth. And if she knew that to be true, then most likely she knew who did kill the man.

"Okay," I said. "But you know I'm going to need proof of that, right? Especially with her doing a runner when I showed up to talk with her."

She looked away and nodded. "Celia was with me when George was killed. Is that enough?"

As I said, I've been doing this kind of thing for a very long time. I can usually tell when someone is lying and when they are telling the truth. Or at least the truth as they know it.

And right now, all my senses were telling me that the woman wasn't lying about being with Celia. Which brought up a very interesting train of thought. Reaching into the case file I'd brought into the room with me, I drew out the image of Celia standing over

George's body and slid it across the table toward her.

She cringed and looked away.

"You and I both know who that wolf is when she turns back into skin form." Her eyes still wouldn't meet mine. I softened my voice. "So, where were you when this picture was taken?"

Flora's gaze traveled briefly to the image and then away again. I could tell she was debating with herself. I could only hope that the woman would make the right choice and talk to me.

It was the only way I could help her.

Chapter 16

There was another long silence. Goddess help me, but I was about ready to break it myself when Flora finally spoke.

"He knew about werewolves." Her eyes finally met mine. "I don't know how he knew, but he knew."

"I'm more curious right now as to how you know he knew."

She swallowed and turned away again. "He was preying on the women werewolves. George wasn't just toting a gun these days. He was carrying a camera, too. And he had all these stupid little surveillance cams set up around the woods, too."

Of all the things I had suspected, this was not one of them.

"Are you saying that he was blackmailing the women?" I paused. "And if it was blackmail, why was he just going after the women?"

Her gaze flitted to me and then away again.

"Because it wasn't money he was after."

Oh, Goddess, no.

"Who was he blackmailing?" Even I could hear the ice in my voice.

She shook her head. "I don't think I'm willing to give out names, you know? They're innocent in all this. They're the true victims here, not George. He deserved what he got."

I reached across the table and covered her hand with mine. "And I'm a werewolf, too, remember? Plus, I'm the only one that can help you all out of this mess. But you have to come straight with me." I waited until she gave a small shiver, then nodded. "What happened that night?"

"Celia and Emma were at my place that night. I didn't mention Celia before when you asked where I was, because she'd asked us not to. I don't know why." She paused, her fingers tracing an imaginary line on the table between us. "We were trying to come up with a plan to stop George. In the middle of our little meeting, my brother came home in a rage."

She took a deep breath. "He's been dating a girl from the Bear's Creek pack. They had been to the park for a run, but then they had a fight. He was totally ticked off at her, so he left her there, stranded."

"Why would he do that with George targeting female weres?"

Flora squirmed a little in her chair. "The men didn't know about it. We were afraid that if they found out, they'd do something…"

"Like kill the man?"

She nodded. "Yeah. Didn't really work, did it?"

"The three of you went to the park to get her, didn't you?"

Another nod. "Unfortunately, my sterling brother had stopped for a drink or two before coming home. We were too late."

"George was already dead when you got there?"

"Yes…" She stopped.

There was more to the story. But whatever it was, she wasn't wanting to share. Unfortunately, at this point, she had to.

"I have to know everything if I'm going to help you."

"When we got there, George was lying there under the tree. I swear he was already dead. But… well, Celia kind of lost it for a minute. All the trouble the man had already caused us, and now we had to deal with this?"

I could read between the lines. Those bite marks on the man had come from Celia's wolf form. Being an Alpha wolf meant something. It must have torn at her to know that she hadn't done her job in protecting her pack. That was probably why she hadn't used the two women as alibis. She'd known that if DNA from George was traced back to her, it would bring them into it, too. She'd been protecting them. My estimation of Celia actually went up a notch.

Then again, if the girl was from Bear's Creek, she wouldn't have been from Celia's pack. And just like that, my heart went cold.

"Your brother's girlfriend was Nell Adams." I made it a statement, not a question. I was that sure of it.

"Yeah."

"Did she kill George?" Goddess help me, but I was really hoping that the answer would be yes. If it was, then we were most likely talking flat-out self-defense. No court in the world would convict her for that.

Flora shrugged. "I don't know. As I said, we were too late."

"Was Nell gone when you got there?"

She hesitated for a minute. "Yes."

"But you said your brother stranded her there without a ride. How did she leave?"

Her eyes were glued on that imaginary traced line on the table. "She must have called someone while my worthless brother was having his drinks."

"Then you probably passed them on the road. Didn't you?"

She swallowed. Yeah, they'd passed them all right.

"Who did Nell call, Flora?"

Her voice was barely a whisper, but I still heard her answer. "Her father, Donnie Adams."

Crapsnackles to infinity and beyond. Now we had a wolf hunt on our hands.

With the whole scent-bomb thing that Donnie had done to cover their tracks, a wolf hunt wouldn't be a simple matter. At all. Unless…

I locked eyes with Flora. "Does your brother have anything of Nell's that would have her scent on it?"

She blinked and looked away. I could tell she didn't want to answer. Not that I could give her that option. Finally, she swallowed and nodded.

"All I can say in his defense is to remind you that he didn't know about the George thing."

What? And then it hit me. "By the Creator, he took her clothes when he left her there, didn't he?"

Another quick nod.

When all of this was said and done, and I'd found Nell and her father, young Mr. Johnson would definitely be having a karma spell thrown his way. I might even get Opal Ravenswind to cast it herself. She was the master of those kinds of spells.

And Flora's brother would deserve anything and everything the spell threw at him, too.

***

At least now I had a scent to work with. That

helped. With one of my issues, anyway.

The other issue wasn't so easily dealt with. Who to include on the wolf hunt.

If this were a manhunt involving a large area like we would be dealing with, there would be an entire team on it. Maybe even a couple of teams. Joint cooperation between law enforcement districts and everything.

That couldn't happen in this case, though. Donnie Adams was smart. He had to know just how big of a hamper he was putting on us finding them when he'd decided to go furry.

Still, I couldn't very well go alone, either. There were two of them and only one of me.

No, I wasn't afraid of them overpowering me. I was dang good at my job, and I had magic to back me up. The problem was in logistics.

Say I found them and they both took off in different directions? I needed both of them to get this thing resolved. And it would make things a heck of a lot simpler if I could nab them both at the same time.

All that to say, I needed a partner. Gray was the obvious choice. It would take a wolf to have any chance of catching them if they ran. And let's face it, the chances were off the charts good that they'd run. Shoot, they'd already run once. Why would they stop now?

Trevor would be my second choice, but unfortunately, this hunt meant I would likely be gone from the station for a few days. With Trevor being my backup, it made little sense to take him with me. I would need him here to hold down the fort.

The problem I was having was my agreement with Steve Brighton. I'd agreed to let him in on the investigation. An agreement I was strongly regretting at the moment.

Agents of the Luparri were masters of the wolf hunt. He'd make a superb partner. That much wasn't in question.

The only trouble with bringing Steve in on the hunt was that once a Luparri agent had their wolf, that tended to be the wolf's last living day on earth. The Luparri acted as judge, jury, and executioner.

And yes, I was second-guessing my entire relationship with Steve at this point. I wanted to trust my heart that he was different, but my mind was stuck on the whole Luparri thing.

In the end, I did what I had to do. The two of us had made a deal, and an honest person would honor it. Even if it would make that hunt twice as dangerous and nerve-wracking as it already would be.

I made the call.

"Hey, Steve, we need to talk."

Chapter 17

It wasn't exactly the kind of conversation one had over the phone. Even if you didn't count on the fact that I wanted to be in a position to watch Steve like a hawk once I gave him the news.

All I'd told him over the phone was that I had a solid lead, and it was all going to boil down to a manhunt that could last a few days. Shoot, as good as Donnie Adams was, it could go even longer than that.

Steve had said he was in for sure, and we'd made plans to meet for supper at my place. And no, I didn't plan to cook. There just wasn't time in my schedule for that. By the time I had arranged with Trevor and the department for my extended absence and packed the essentials that I thought I'd need for the trip, seeing Steve with those wonderful-smelling Chinese takeout bags was a very welcome sight indeed.

As we munched, I filled him in. On everything. And just maybe I went a little heavy on the self-defense angle of it, but I was fairly certain that's what it had been. Whether Nell had been the one to pull that trigger or her father, either way, it was justified. At least, it was to my way of thinking.

I was betting a jury would feel the same way. If it came to that.

"Let me get this straight," Steve said slowly. "George was blackmailing female werewolves for sexual favors?"

"That's what I've been told. It pretty much keeps in character with the man's history, too."

He let out a long breath. "I really wish Donnie and Nell hadn't run. This could have been handled much easier if they'd just come to you with this."

"Preaching to the choir, Steve." I paused for another bite of my lo mien. I loved those stupid noodles. "But we're talking about a father and his daughter here. I'm going to bet that he ran to protect her."

"Which means she could have been the one to pull that trigger. Making the self-defense thing a shoo-in verdict."

I shrugged. "Maybe. Or maybe the man didn't like Nell's chances of a life without him in it. If he went to jail, the girl would be on her own. Or put into foster care. And George isn't the only pervert out there."

"True."

Silence fell as we finished our meal. Towards

the end, I looked over the now empty containers at him. "I'm planning to head out at daybreak tomorrow. You're welcome to spend the night here if you want."

"Thanks. I'll take you up on that."

That made my night a whole lot easier, for sure. If he had left, I'd have had to follow him. I wasn't kidding about that watching him like a hawk thing.

"Your department give you any trouble about the time off work?" I mean, this wasn't like it was an active case for Oak Hill, now was it?

He wasn't meeting my eyes. I didn't like that. "Steve?"

"I quit. And before you say anything, I knew this day would come, eventually." He paused. "With the salary the Luparii pays me, I really don't need a second job. It just makes it easier to blend in if I have one. But sometimes that's hard to manage with the time off I require for hunts."

He gave me one of his crooked smiles. "Once this is done, if you know of any suitable part-time jobs available, I'd appreciate a good word."

"I'm sure you can find something." I wasn't about to commit to anything right now. Besides, if I offered Steve a job with my station, well, that opened a whole other can of worms, didn't it? I wasn't at all sure I was ready for that just yet.

The rest of the early evening we spent poring over area maps of the South Branch of Au Sable, noting the best possible long-term campsites. By ten, however, I was ready to call it a night. Daybreak came early, and I hadn't been kidding about that as my starting time for the adventure ahead.

I was about to offer Steve the use of my sleeping bag for the night when he surprised me by bringing his own in from his vehicle. Guess I wasn't the only one packed and ready to go, huh? That kind of made sense now that I thought about it. Otherwise, the man wouldn't have been up to spending the night, would he? He'd have had packing to do.

"One quick question before we turn in for the night," he said. "Is Donnie's truck still there?"

"Yup. The locals are keeping an eye on it for us. Not a stakeout or anything like that, but we'd know if it had been moved."

"So we're sure they're still there then."

I nodded. "As sure as we can be." It was possible that Donnie had dumped the truck there to throw us off the trail and then hitched a ride with a friend. But from everything Gray had told me, Donnie was more the lone wolf kind of guy. It had taken Gray a long time to get him and Nell into the pack.

For the record, I really hoped I wasn't making a colossal mistake by taking Steve rather than Gray on this hunt. I'd love to have had them both, but I didn't feel right asking Gray to give up his secret to a member of the Luparii.

Not yet, anyway.

***

It didn't take us long to find the Adams' truck once we hit the preserve area. The local directions were spot on. That helped.

I was still walking around the vehicle when I noticed Steve reaching for the door handle.

"No!" I shouted.

He jerked back and stared at me. "What the heck?"

I cleared my throat and tried to get my heartbeat back down. There had been a reason I'd warned the locals not to try to enter the abandoned vehicle.

"When I went to Donnie and Nell's house, they had booby-trapped it with a scent bomb. I can't take the risk of having that happen a second time."

I meant that, too. It had taken my scenting abilities a long time to recover from the last one. And I needed that ability for this hunt. At least, in the beginning.

That's what made me fairly certain that Donnie would have booby-trapped the vehicle, too. He had to have known that eventually the truck would be found and that the news would get back to me.

And he knew exactly who and what I was, too. He'd be ready for that.

Steve was looking from the truck to me and

then back. "Is there any way to neutralize it? There might be something inside that would be of use to us."

"Donnie Adams knows his way around a scent bomb, believe me. I can't take the risk." Which brought up a very useful thought. "I don't know how the Luparri track their prey, but we wolves track by scent. That thing goes off, and I'm out of the game for a good twenty-four hours."

Or longer, but I didn't exactly want to come across as the weak link here, now did I?

Steve hesitated a second longer, then turned away from the truck. I breathed a lot easier after that.

"Okay, so what is our first move?"

I pulled out Nell's clothes from my backpack. I'd had them sealed separately in plastic bags to preserve the scent as best I could.

"Now we track." I paused. "But it might help me to know exactly how you work a wolf hunt. Maybe we can combine our strengths here?"

I really didn't like the long hesitation that followed my suggestion. If Steve thought we could work together and him still keep all his Luparri secrets, then we'd just run into our first snag. I was being upfront and open with him, dang it all.

And I expected the same in return, too.

Finally, he took a deep breath and broke. "We don't use scent." He pointed to his nose. "Normal human sniffer here. Not all that great for much, I'm afraid."

I blinked at him. "Then how do you track wolves?"

He shrugged. "The old-fashioned way. The way any human hunter tracks his prey."

Oh. I was beginning to see why Steve had wanted to team up with me so badly. Tracking a couple of wolves in a nature preserve that was over three thousand acres? Yeah, a day or two wouldn't even scratch the surface.

Guess I wasn't the weak link in our partnership, after all, now was I?

Especially when you considered that if the scent trail ran cold, I still had an ace up my sleeve.

Chapter 18

If I had been alone on this, or with Trevor or Gray, I'd have gone straight with the Find spell. But I wasn't alone. I was on a joint hunt. With a member of the Luparri, no less.

Steve knew I was a wolf, and he knew about the whole witch thing, too. The thing was, a lot of people thought being a witch was simply a lifestyle choice. Kind of like choosing a religion.

We didn't tend to try to dissuade them from that notion much, either. If they knew the true power of Elemental witches, they would feel far differently about us. Or at least, that was my greatest fear.

Even if I was only half Elemental. With the other half being a werewolf, it really didn't put me in a better place, now did it?

All that having been said, Steve already thought I was different. I really didn't want to show the man just how different I truly was unless it became absolutely necessary. The Luparri weren't all that well known for liking 'different'. And even after I'd brewed that secrecy potion—and he'd drank it—I still didn't think that he truly believed a witch had any real power. That would change pretty fast if he ever tried to betray one of my pack to the Luparii.

And besides, there was a chance following a scent trail would work… wasn't there?

It took an enormous amount of trust on my part to change form in the presence of a Luparri. Even if he was facing the other way at the time. As a wolf, a lot of the self-defense mechanisms that a witch had available to her were rendered useless. It made me feel… vulnerable, to say the least.

Not that a wolf didn't have the ability to defend themselves. They did. Wolves are awesome, trust me.

The trouble is, none of those abilities were much good if the person presenting the danger was any distance away. So yeah, a heck of a lot of trust was being shown on my part here. I only hoped that Steve realized that.

Taking a deep breath, I nudged the back of his knee to let him know I was ready. His head whipped around and then down to look at me, his eyes widening when he got his first glance at my furred form.

I could handle the widened eyes, but the brief glimpse of fear in them just about made my heart go into palpitations. I had hoped he would be past the fear stage. It would appear that knowing someone was a werewolf was far different from actually seeing that they were a werewolf with your own eyes.

At least, that appeared to be the case with Steve. Luckily, he recovered pretty quickly. Clearing his throat, he asked, "You ready to go?"

I chuffed, then walked over and nudged the small pile of my discarded clothing with my nose.

He cleared his throat again. "I need to take your clothes with us, don't I?"

I just looked at him. It was hard to get emotion across when you're a wolf. So a cocked head would just have to do.

Steve chuckled. "Okay, I get it. That was a stupid question, wasn't it?"

You know… this just might work after all. At least that might have been true if we'd been after anyone other than Donnie Adams.

The truck was the obvious starting point. Unfortunately, the time that had passed since that truck had been parked didn't help our cause. The scent had faded greatly. But luckily, my alpha-wolf-super-snout was up to the task.

We followed their trail the entire morning, and into the afternoon. We spent a lot of that time backtracking and looping. Again, Donnie Adams knew how to go to ground.

A fact that became doubly apparent around mid-afternoon when I started sneezing.

I'm not talking just a simple sneeze or two to clear my sinuses, either. I'm talking about a long, drawn-out sneezing fit. One that didn't end until I took pity on my wolfy form and changed back into a human.

A naked human.

Steve and I hadn't taken that step in our relationship yet. Now, I'd forever have to live with the fact that his first glimpse of my human naked form was during a sneezing fit. Not exactly what I would have chosen in the way of timing.

His cheeks colored slightly, but he took it in stride, digging in his pack and handing me my clothes. I jogged a little distance away before taking the time to dress. My human nose wasn't as good at scent as my wolf one, but it was still much, much better than the average human snout.

Steve gave me a minute, then followed me into the trees.

"What happened back there?"

I held up my hand as I felt one last sneeze making its way to the surface. Once that one had passed, I could breathe easier again.

"Pepper. Tons and tons of Cayenne Pepper."

He let that sink in for a minute. "You think you can pick the trail back up a little way from here?"

I thought about it. There was a chance I could do just that. There was an even better chance that I'd get another snout full of pepper while trying to make that happen. That really wasn't a chance I wanted to take.

Whether I liked it or not, the time had come.

Steve had met two parts of the total me. Human and wolf. He was about to meet the third in full action.

It was time to cast that dang Find spell.

***

The good thing about Find spells is that they take out all the looping around and backtracking. They don't follow the path a person took. They just showed you the most direct path to the person you were seeking.

Unfortunately, that was also the bad thing about Find spells. The spell didn't much care if there was a tree or a big hill in the way. One had to go around, or up and over, as the case may be.

For the record, Steve was handling the witch thing better than I would have thought. If he had doubts about my sudden certainty on the direction to go, he was keeping them to himself. I appreciated that. Normals couldn't see the thin blue line of magic that I was following. That meant he was taking it all on faith.

Faith in me. That meant something.

It took both of the girl's socks to find her. When the first spell fizzled out, I cast the second. And yes, when I cast it, I said a little prayer to the Goddess that we would find them before we ran out of clothing to use.

My sinuses couldn't take another pepper beating. And I wasn't all that much wanting to take the time to track them the old-fashioned way. I'm sure we could have done it, but dang, it would have taken days.

It took us about three-quarters of an hour with my magic. When I saw the blue line end in the center of a clearing with nothing else around it, I held up my arm, stopping Steve from going forward.

He looked at me. "A trap?" he mouthed.

I shook my head. Then thought better about it. "Maybe," I whispered. "I think they're underground now."

Steve looked from the clearing to me and back again. "What makes you say that?"

At times like this, I kind of wished the regulars could see that line of magic. "The spell says that Nell Adams is in the center of that clearing. And my Find spells don't lie."

His face cleared as he nodded. "He's dug them a shelter. Smart."

I had to agree. And knowing Donnie Adams' reputation for outdoor survival, he'd probably had this place all ready to go as a fallout shelter. Which meant he probably had a lot of supplies down there with them.

They might be able to hold out down there for days. Weeks, even.

Which really only left us with two options. Go in after them—not the safest option by far—or wait them out.

The trouble was, I was never much good at the waiting thing.

Chapter 19

Next up is where my new partner had his time to shine. And shine he did.

My Find spell might have located Nell Adams, well and truly, but it didn't show us the way to get to her. That way wasn't immediately apparent, either. The area above where my spell's blue line ended was nothing more than solid soil and grass. No way in or down.

As Steve did his thing, it became more and more clear that this wasn't a hastily thrown together bolt hole. This thing had taken time and a heck of a lot of energy, too. He'd probably been working on this for years. And it showed.

As we were looking for the entrance, we discovered a few 'air holes' spaced judiciously around the area. From the look of it, we weren't talking about a small little dwelling hole here. That was probably one reason it was so far off the beaten path. Not too many tourists branch off the main paths here. Too easy to get lost.

This was well off any of those paths. Probably didn't get much ranger activity out here, either. Which, of course, only made the area even more perfect for Donnie Adams to construct this in relative privacy.

I'm not sure I would ever have found the entrance. Or smelled it, either, as there was more than a trace smell of pepper in the air. I could smell it even in human form. Didn't make me want to go furry any time soon. My poor nose had suffered enough in this investigation.

Standing over the elaborately constructed and camouflaged entrance, Steve stared at me from the other side.

"So what's the plan now?" he asked in a whisper. "Wait them out?"

I grunted. "How much time have you got?"

"Good point." He scratched his chin. "What are the chances of us going down and coming back up alive?"

Yeah, that was the question, all right. The other question was… what if there was another entrance that we hadn't found yet? Somehow, I just couldn't see Adams only giving himself one way out. Shoot, there could be a couple more we hadn't found yet. That sounded more like the man.

Trouble was, it had taken us a few hours of painstaking effort just to find this one. And I was growing very tired of this cat-and-mouse game. Not to mention the fact that it would be dark soon.

Yes, we had the ability and supplies to make it one night without retreating to the vehicle. But I didn't want to have to spend the night out in the open unless I absolutely had to.

Which again left me with two choices. Very narrow number, two. I could cast a stealth spell and try to sneak up on them, or I could yell down the hole and announce my presence first. Either way had its drawbacks.

After a minute of silent debate with myself, I looked over at Steve. "You stay up here. I'm betting this isn't the only entrance, and they're likely to head for another exit when they see me." My eyes bore into his. "No shooting, you hear me? Just detain them until I make it out after them. Can you promise me that?"

That was the sticking point with me. I trusted Steve Brighton, the man. The trust jury was still out for Steve Brighton, the Luparri agent.

He nodded. "If I have to shoot, it'll be a tranquilizer dart. You have my word."

So be it. I took a deep breath, cast the stealth spell along with a night vision one, and crawled into the hole.

Goddess help me.

***

It was at times like this that I regretted my questionable hybrid status as half wolf and half witch. Wolves live in dens. And yes, most of the time, those dens are dug out of soft soil. They're technically underground. The wolf part of me didn't have an issue with crawling into that hole.

The human and witch part of me, however, did. I liked small spaces, yes. That is evident from my tiny home lifestyle. But crawling into that hole made me realize that maybe an earth berm house like the Adams' lived in might not be right for me, after all.

Unfortunately, I was an enforcer of the law after a quarry. As such, I really had little choice in the matter.

At least it wasn't as dark as I had imagined it would be. That's because Adams was even more prepared than I had thought. The man even had lighting installed down here. Simple pushbutton lights were spread out along the reinforced ceiling of the tunnel. One every ten feet.

Not enough to make it bright as day down here, but that was more than fine with me. I didn't really want them to have the advantage of seeing me coming from far off. Of course, the stealth spell should help with that. But sooner or later, I was going to have to announce my presence.

That was the part that worried me.

If Adams had, oh say a shotgun, all he'd have to do would be point the end of the barrel toward my end of the tunnel, and my days on earth would be over. End of story. Hasta la vista, Patty Bluespring.

All I could do was hope that wouldn't be the case. I was counting on Donnie Adams being reasonable. After all, he had to know I had a job to do here. If he would just let me, I might be able to get them out of this mess fairly easily.

As long as things truly had gone down with George Vincent the way I was figuring they had. You're allowed by law to protect yourself and your family. If you weren't, well, I wouldn't be the law.

Around twenty-five feet in, the tunnel seemed to end. At least it did from where I was currently crawling. I was assuming that it would branch off either to the left or the right at that point. If my somewhat addled brain was remembering the situation up top correctly, it would go to the left.

Unless, of course, we'd found a dummy hole. Or, even worse, a trap.

Crap.

It had been hard enough to put one hand in front of the other this far, but now it was even harder. Donnie Adams loved his traps. All the possible scenarios ran through my head as I stopped to ponder the situation.

The only thing that got me started again was Gray's opinion that Donnie Adams was a good man. A good man wouldn't try to hurt innocent people, would he? And even if he did have a somewhat justifiable reason for running, he would have to know that those coming after him would be innocent.

Technically, he'd have to know that the one coming after him would be me.

I took another couple of deep breaths and crawled on. At that point, I would have given just about anything to change into wolf form. For one thing, it wouldn't have been nearly as cramped in that stupid tunnel. My furry form is smaller than my human one.

But I couldn't afford to do that. Wolves could communicate with each other—in a fashion. What we couldn't do was talk. I needed that ability to try to break through to Donnie's sense of reason. Nell's, too, for that matter.

I fully realized just how much they stood to possibly lose here. Hopefully, I could get them to see that life on the run wasn't really much of a life. Especially for a teenage girl. For that, I needed words.

Unfortunately, I was still thinking just what those words might be when two very important things happened at once.

One, I heard voices just to the left, right before I hit the end of the tunnel. Good thing, too, because as luck would have it, the tunnel branched off to the right as well as to the left. But that was where my luck ended.

Because the second thing that happened?

I hit another of Donnie Adams' traps.

As soon as I felt the ground shift under my left hand, I knew I'd made a misstep. Or a mis-crawl, as it were. And boy oh boy had I ever.

The shifting ground was a trigger that activated a series of events. I have very quick reflexes. Unfortunately, even as I scurried backward toward the entrance, the trap released.

There must have been a connecting line between the trigger and a rifle set up down the right side of the tunnel ahead. And pointed straight at me.

The right tunnel, for reasons that were now rather obvious to me, wasn't lit. So there hadn't been an opportunity to see the gun before it fired. The missile almost missed me.

Almost. If I'd been a split second faster, my chances would have been much greater.

Chapter 20

If it had been a bullet, I might have gotten by with a flesh wound. As it was, when I came around, it was to the sight of a dart sticking out of my right arm. Trust a good man to use a tranquilizer dart rather than a deadly round. At least Gray had been right about that part.

I pulled the dart out and tossed it to the side, then raced forward into the unknown.

Yes, I could have gone backward toward the entrance I'd come in through. But turning around in these cramped quarters would have taken time. Plus, I knew that no one could have fit to get past me in this tight tunnel, which meant that Donnie and Nell had to have used an alternate exit.

I got lucky that there weren't any more traps between me and that second exit, because I couldn't afford to take things slow to test the waters. The two wolves might have popped up from an unexpected spot, but I had no doubt that Steve would have been prepared for that to happen.

The good news was, the second exit was a lot closer to their little lair than the first one. It only took me seconds to reach it and gain access once again to the outside world.

I shoved myself through the hole and then immediately rolled to the side. It would be just like Donnie to have another trap set here. But if he did have, I was lucky enough to miss it.

"About time you joined us," Steve said.

I looked up to see him grinning at me. Surely he wouldn't be grinning if things hadn't gone well… would he?

"The Adams'?"

He stepped to the side so that I could better see the scene behind him. Donnie and Nell were propped up on opposite sides of a medium-sized tree. Their hands were handcuffed on either side to each other. They wouldn't be going anywhere without taking that tree with them.

Shifting wouldn't do them a bit of good, either. In fact, it might hurt more than a little, depending on the size of their wolf legs and feet. Handcuffs weren't very forgiving.

I fell over to the side, letting the wave of relief pass through me. Steve hadn't betrayed my trust. There wouldn't have been any need to handcuff two dead bodies together. They were alive and well, if knocked out.

And after having been through that little episode myself—at their hands—I didn't feel one little bit sorry for them on that one.

Steve reached a hand down to me. I took it and stood.

"Sorry I didn't make it down to check on you. I had to get them situated first. I kind of figured you'd be more than a little upset with me if I let them get away at this point."

I nodded. "Good call." Then I glanced up at the sky as I rubbed my right arm. It was still tingling. "How long was I down there?"

He shrugged. "I'd say ten minutes, tops. I heard a muffled popping noise about two minutes in, then these two sprung up out of nowhere." He shook his head and chuckled. "Donnie Adams is very, very good."

I grinned at him. "But you're better."

Another shrug. "Well, yeah, obviously."

"Dad?" Nell's voice had more than a little fear and anxiety in it. She couldn't see him from where she was situated.

And yes, Steve had earned a bit more of my trust, too. The two of them weren't naked. They should have been, unless they'd been in human form down in that hole, and I really didn't think they had been. As I've said, human forms take up more space. Plus, they were both more wolf than I was.

Nell was wearing a long and very oversized t-shirt, and Donnie was in a baggy pair of sweatpants. The main thing was, all their most private parts were covered. Steve had given them the decency of that.

I appreciated that more than he knew. It spoke to the kind of man he really was.

"I'm here," Donnie said. He tested the handcuffs, then gave up and leaned back against the tree, his eyes seeking me out. "Guess you got us, Sheriff, but it isn't what you think."

It was harder than it should have been to smile at the man, what with my arm still tingling and part numb, but I managed. If I'd been in his shoes, I'd have probably done the same dang thing. Or something very similar, at the least.

I added a cocked eyebrow to my smile. "You mean one of you didn't, in fact, shoot George Vincent in self-defense?"

He blinked at me for a minute. "Okay, so maybe it was what you think. How'd you work it out?"

"I'm just that good, I guess." I paused. "It would have been a lot easier on all of us if you'd both just come to me in the first place, you know."

He nodded. "Sorry about that. Maybe I wasn't thinking too clearly."

Yeah, right. I rather thought it would take a very clear head to have accomplished the getaway he had. But why argue that point now?

At my nod, Steve unfastened the first set of handcuffs from Nell's wrist, then he immediately clasped the loose end on his own wrist. I reached out, and he handed me the key. I did the same on Donnie's other wrist, connecting me with Nell.

"Okay," I told them as we all moved out into the clearing. "Here is what I want to happen. I want the two of you to tell me exactly how and why you killed George Vincent. If your stories line up with the truth I've uncovered so far, then I think we can put this to bed pretty easily. But I want the truth." My eyes bore into Donnie's own. "Do I make myself clear?"

He nodded, then looked over at Nell. "The truth is our best option now, girl. Sheriff Bluespring is fair. We lucked out that she's the sheriff now. She'll understand the situation better than most."

Nell didn't look all that sure, but she nodded. She still hadn't looked up at me. Her long, dark hair covered her face. It made me wish I had a ponytail holder. But with my own short hair, I never had need of them.

Normally, I would have separated the two to get clearer stories out of them. But at this point, that ship had sailed. They'd had far too much time together to get their stories straight by now. They probably even had them memorized.

I didn't care. As long as they were true stories.

We sat down opposite each other on the

ground, just out of reach. Donnie opened his mouth, but I held up a hand.

"Sorry, Donnie, but I think I want to hear Nell's version first."

Nell did look up at that—straight into her father's eyes. He nodded. "Just tell the truth, girl."

Her head went back down, making me wish again for a rubber band, something that would let me see the girl's face as she talked.

"It started out as a date… or it was supposed to be." Her eyes darted to her father and then back down at the ground. "Dad didn't like the boy I was seeing, so I met him at the end of the drive and he drove us to that park in Wind's Crossing. We were supposed to go for a run and then cuddle up afterward, only…"

"Only you got into a fight instead?" I asked. I mean, I already knew that much, didn't I?

She nodded. "Yeah. He took my clothes and left me there."

Donnie's hands bunched into fists. "You know you're going to have to give me that boy's name sooner or later, don't you?"

Nell looked at me for the first time.

"It's okay. I know who it was," I told her. Then I looked over at Donnie. "And believe me when I say he's vastly regretting that decision by now." I mean, I was pretty sure his sister and the rest of the women in the pack had seen to that.

"Not as much as he's gonna when I get my hands on him," Donnie said.

I cocked my head at him. "Don't you think your daughter had been through enough already? You really want to leave her alone to go through this mess while you sit in one of my cells on an assault charge?"

He grunted but didn't say anything. I'd take that grunt as a sign that he understood what I was saying.

"What happened after that?" I asked, lifting Nell's chin so that I could actually see her face. We were coming to the important part now, and dang it all, I wanted to see those eyes of hers.

She shivered and swallowed. "Well, I always kept my phone on me. I have an expandable harness that works with both forms. So the first thing I did was call Dad to come get me."

"And then?"

Her shivering increased. Most of that was nerves. I got that. But part of it was the cool breeze and the fact that the sun was starting to go down. I held up a hand and dug in my pack for a minute, pulling out a pair of jeans.

It made a lot more sense to let her wear her clothes rather than me keep carry them around. I didn't need them for scent any longer. I had my prey.

She gave me a grateful smile and slid into them.

"Maybe we should continue this as we walk

toward the car?" Steve suggested. "The going will be a lot easier if we still have light to see."

The man had a good point.

Chapter 21

By the time we made it back to the car—and truck—I had the full story of that night's fateful events.

It all amounted to nothing more than poor timing. George had been out for a bit of wolf hunting at the park. Now that he knew it was a werewolf hangout—and that werewolves really existed, mind you—he'd been haunting the place, looking for more women to blackmail into his bidding.

Who knows? Maybe he'd even come up with a plan to get the males involved in the blackmail scheme, too, but I doubted it. A man like George wouldn't be likely to take that big of a risk.

He must have had the scope of his rifle on the pair of wolves right as they turned back to human form because he bided his time until the boy left the girl alone and defenseless. Unfortunately for him, Nell was her father's daughter.

She had skills that your normal teenage girl just didn't have. Survival skills and fighting skills. George hadn't been expecting that. She'd managed to get the man's rifle pretty easily, according to her, but then when she tried to back away to wait for her dad to show up, he lunged at her and grabbed for the gun.

As her finger was already on the trigger for safety's sake, the rough tug he gave the gun was enough to finish the job. To my mind, in a way, you couldn't even say that Nell had pulled the trigger. George had kind of pulled it from his end—the wrong end, as it turned out.

The fact is, I believed her. It fit with what I already knew about the night and George. That didn't mean we didn't head straight for my lock-up, because we did.

I was pretty sure the two of them wouldn't face any truly serious charges, but there was the fact that they ran to consider. And I couldn't very well hide that fact, now could I? Not when I'd had to arrange time off from the station to track them both down.

So they spent the night in my lockup. The next morning, I had the pleasure of explaining the situation to the prosecutor, minus all the wolfy stuff, obviously. Donnie lucked out, as the man had a teenage daughter of his own. I didn't think it was all that hard for him to put himself in Donnie's shoes as a father. That helped.

By that time, Damon Nichols had already

called and told me their pack's intention to bail the two of them out if and when that option became available. Part of that may have been Damon's cunning to get me to show Celia a little leniency once I got my hands on her. Either way, I'd take it.

I kind of hoped that maybe this would bring the two packs a little closer together. It was for sure a gesture of goodwill, at any rate. Of course, if the young male wolf from our pack hadn't left Nell naked and vulnerable, things might not have come to this. Part of this was on him, and Damon and the pack acknowledged that fact in full.

And hopefully, they'd have that option of bail very soon. At least they would if the prosecutor kept his word to me. The only charge being brought against them at this time would be obstruction of justice. Most likely, they'd get by with a light probation and no time served.

Well, other than the one night they'd already spent in my jail.

It was a good ending, I thought. I'd take all of those that I could get. And the ending wasn't just good for the Adams family either.

It was good for me.

As much as I liked Steve Brighton, part of me had always been afraid to actually commit to a physical relationship. That fear was no longer there.

It was time to take us to the next level as a couple.

And yes, he seemed more than okay with that idea.

###

Books by Belinda White

Accidental Familiar Series

All Too Familiar
Relatively Familiar
Un-Familiar Magic
Home Familiar Home
A Familiar Tail
Familiar Beginnings (Prequel)

Gemstone Coven Holiday Shorts

A Very Opal Halloween
A Very Happy Birthday Halloween

Witch Reborn Series

Witch of a Godmother
Witch of a Sister
Witch of a Bride
Witch of an Ex
Witch of a Honeymoon
Witch of a Neighbor
Witch of a Mother

Yorkie Doodle Mysteries (Novellas)

Yorkie Doodle Dandy

Spell and Protect

Yorkie Doodle Sweetheart
Yorkie Doodle Joy

Team Destiny Paranormal Cozy Mystery Series

Team Destiny and Gray's Grave
Team Destiny and Archie's Apparition
Team Destiny and Shaman's Secret
Team Destiny and Trevor's Tarot
Team Destiny and Opal's Obligation
Team Destiny and Patty's Probation

Benandanti Series (Wolves)

Finders Weepers
Sister's Keepers
Demon Peepers

9 7 9 8 8 3 9 6 2 7 7 1 0